D0930577

A GUN FOR JOHNNY DEERE

**Center Point
Large Print**

**This Large Print Book carries the
Seal of Approval of N.A.V.H.**

ॐ श्री गणेशाय नमः

A GUN FOR JOHNNY DEERE

WAYNE D. OVERHOLSER

CENTER POINT PUBLISHING
THORNDIKE, MAINE

This Center Point Large Print edition
is published in the year 2001 by arrangement with
Golden West Literary Agency.

The text of this Large Print edition is unabridged.
In other aspects, this book may vary from the original edition.
Printed in Thailand. Set in 16-point
Times New Roman type by Bill Coskrey.

ISBN 1-58547-100-3

Library of Congress Cataloging-in-Publication Data

Overholser, Wayne D., 1906-
    A gun for Johnny Deere / Wayne D. Overholser.
      p. cm.
    ISBN 1-58547-100-3 (lib. bdg. : alk. paper)
    1. Large type books. I. Title.

PS3529.V33 G775 2001
813'.54--dc21

                                        2001028485

Johnny Deere was always reckless when he rode into Star City on a Saturday afternoon, reckless enough to make his father worry about him until he got back home sometime Sunday morning. Now, topping the last ridge south of town, he looked down into the valley that held a cluster of buildings and the cottonwoods that shaded them, and he felt the recklessness grow in him until the tension was unbearable and he had to holler just to relieve it.

"The juices of life," his father had often told him, "are bubbling in you like they was boiling on a hot stove. That's fine 'cause it's natural for 'em to boil when you're young. When I was twenty-one, I reckon I was the same way. Only thing is you've got to be careful they don't boil so hard you get into a pot of trouble you can't get out of."

Right now he didn't much care whether he got into trouble or not. He pulled his gun and fired at the sky and let out the holler, then he holstered the gun and went past the cemetery and down the long slope to town on the run, the buckskin's hoofs leaving a dust cloud all the way back to the ridge top. It wasn't just the juices of life that made him reckless, he told himself. Anybody but his father would go crazy living the way they did back there in the sand hills and not

5

seeing anybody else for maybe a month at a time.

He hit the bridge that spanned Pole Creek, the buckskin's hoofs striking the planks with sounds that were as sharp as pistol reports in the sultry August afternoon. Ahead of him above the cottonwoods was the water tower with the words WATCH STAR CITY GROW so weathered that they were hard to read. When he was a boy the letters were black and clear and he could read them from the top of the ridge south of town.

Making the sharp left-hand turn onto Main Street, he looked down the dust strip with the broken board-walks on both sides and the business buildings that needed painting, half of them empty, and he let out another whoop as he reined into Linda Hollison's front yard. He hadn't aimed to make the holler this time and he hadn't planned to turn into Linda's yard, either, but he'd done both and he knew why. Star City was dead and decaying, and if he didn't let on he was alive, they'd maybe bury him back up there on the ridge before he knew it.

Linda ran out of the house as he swung down. She yelled: "What do you mean, riding in here and hol-lering bloody murder? Is the house on fire?"

He cuffed back his Stetson and wiped a sleeve across his sweaty face, then stood frowning as if studying over what she'd said. He wasn't. He just liked to look at her. She was seventeen and on the slim side, but she had filled out in the right places. She knew it and she was proud of it just as she was proud of her ability to make a man's blood start pounding in his temples with a swing of her hips.

"No," he said finally. "I just wanted you to know that a man was in town."

"Well, if you ain't the most con . . . ," she began.

He didn't let her finish. He took her into his arms and kissed her. She had the reddest hair he had ever seen and the hottest temper he had ever run into. Always before when he kissed her she had fought like an alley cat, beating at him with her fists or kicking him on the shins, but not today.

When he let her go, she didn't back off or offer to hit him. She was tall for a girl, but she still had to tip her head back to look him in the face. She said, "Thank you kindly for the kiss, but you haven't shaved all week and you smell like a horse. Is that any way to come calling on your girl?"

"My girl?" He blinked and shook his head at her. "Hell and hallelujah, I thought all this time I was trespassing on Tom Tatum's property."

"That's what everybody thinks," she said tartly, "including Tom and Tom's ornery old dad and my mother, but nobody ever asks me. If you've been stopping and kissing me just to get under Tom's hide, you can ride on past next time, but if you want me to be your girl, and if you ain't afraid of Tom . . ."

"I ain't afraid of Tom," he said quickly. "I've licked him a time or two and I can do it again, but I guess maybe I am afraid of old Bull."

"So's everybody else," she said bitterly. "And Sherm Balder. He knows that the minute he bucks old Bull, he'll never get elected sheriff again. But I ain't afraid of him and I hate Tom because he don't never stand up to his dad." She stomped her foot and whirled away from him, her skirt rippling out in a circle away from her trim ankles. She started toward the house, calling back, "Of course if you're afraid of him, too, I guess you ain't as much man . . ."

He ran after her and caught an arm and spun her around. "Now just hold your horses, Red. When I said I was afraid of old Bull, I put myself in the same boat with everybody else just like you said. If you think that makes me less than a man, then I don't want you for my girl."

She smiled, the corners of her mouth trembling. "I want you for my fella," she said, "and I know you're a lot of man or I wouldn't be talking this way. If you want to take me to the dance tonight, why, I'll go with you, but if you don't, quit playing like you've been doing, riding in this way and calling me out of the house and kissing me. The neighbors see you and tell Tom and he bawls me out. It's going to be one way or the other, Johnny. You've got to decide."

"I suppose Tom figures to take you to the

dance tonight?"

"Sure he does, but maybe you'll get here first." She laughed softly. "Either way, first or last, you'll have a fight on your hands and I'll be the cause of it."

He grinned at her. The recklessness that had been briefly tempered by caution was crowding him again. "It's been a dull week. A fight's what I need, and for a pretty girl to boot."

He put his hands on her again and looked down at her; he saw her lips tremble and felt her body stiffen, and she cried out: "Johnny, don't do it. Don't even dream about a girl like me. I'll use you and throw you away when I'm done with you and I'll wind up marrying Tom Tatum."

"I know it," he said, "but it will be a lot of fun while it lasts."

He brought her to him and kissed her again; he felt the fire that was in her kindle a flame in him, and when he let her go, she whispered: "Johnny, it ain't true. I won't throw you away because I'm done with you." She took a long breath, her taut young breasts lifting under her blouse, and she said: "Don't take me to the dance. They'll kill you if you do."

She whirled away from him and ran into the house. He called, "Eight o'clock," but she didn't stop and she didn't look back, and he wasn't sure whether she heard or not.

For a time he stood staring at her front door. She

knew he'd be here tonight, he thought. Then it occurred to him that there was more to this than she had told him. Tom Tatum was Johnny's age, and nothing to be afraid of, but old Bull Tatum was.

Tom's dad was referred to as old Bull, but why it was Johnny didn't know. He was about forty-five, and there was nothing about him that made him seem old. He was big and strong and as ornery as any uncut male critter on his sprawling Rainbow range that ran clean over into Nebraska to the head of the Frenchman.

Johnny stepped into the saddle, thinking there wasn't a man in the Pole Creek country who wasn't afraid of old Bull Tatum and that included Tom as Linda had said. Johnny doubted that Tom was really in love with her. Chances were it was old Bull who had picked her out to be Tom's wife. She was young and strong and a good worker, and to old Bull those were the qualities that counted. Now it was up to Tom to court her and fight off anyone who tried to cut in.

Johnny rode slowly down Main Street to the livery stable, glancing again at the water tower and the weathered words WATCH STAR CITY GROW. In a way it was the words of a dirge, with old Bull Tatum playing the funeral march. The town hadn't grown as long as Johnny could remember. In fact, the population was less than it had been fifteen years ago.

Johnny's father, Frank Deere, and Sherm Balder

had founded the town back in the days when the homestead boom was on. Dakota Sam Weeks who still published the *Star City Clarion* had recited the usual bold promises about Pole Creek Valley being in the rain belt and therefore in time would become one of the great wheat-producing regions of the world.

Dakota Sam had been a little too optimistic. The dry years had come. Along with the Panic of 1893, the drought ran the homesteaders out of the country faster than they had come in. Then old Bull Tatum had moved onto the hard land north of Pole Creek and immediately had started reaching out in all directions as if he were a dry land octopus.

Star City had gone down hill and had never come back. Johnny's father lost his town property and wound up with nothing except his ranch in the sand hills south of Pole Creek. Sherm Balder had done a little better. He had hung onto the sheriff's star, and with the meager salary the county paid, he kept the taxes paid up on his business buildings.

The country would come back, Sherm said repeatedly. The farmers would return and he'd live to see the day when he'd have every building on Main Street rented again. He never got around to saying how he planned to get rid of old Bull Tatum. He knew as well as anyone that old Bull would shoot the first farmer who moved onto Rainbow range.

Well, Sherm didn't have many of his buildings

rented now, Johnny thought, as he reined into Al Frolich's livery stable. Aside from the stable and Dakota Sam Weeks's printshop, the only businesses in town were the blacksmith shop, Doc Allen's drugstore, Harlan Spain's hotel, the barbershop, and Pete Goken's Mercantile.

More often than not, Sherm Balder didn't get his rent money. He couldn't afford to throw anyone out because then the town would lose a business that it needed. The talk was that over the years he had borrowed from old Bull Tatum and this was one of the levers the cowman used to hold Sherm in line.

Al Frolich strode along the runway. When he saw who had come in, he asked, "How's Frank, Johnny?"

"Same as usual," Johnny answered. "He ain't good but he ain't bad, neither. He still does a day's work."

Frolich grunted something, then he asked, "You goin' to the dance?"

"Figgered on it."

"Big shindig. Women been over there in the Oddfellows Hall decorating all day with colored paper and stuff." He wiped a dirty sleeve across a dirty face, his eyes making a careful appraisal of Johnny as if he had a question in mind he wanted to ask, then decided against it. "Sure hot for a dance. You'll be sweating like a horse afore the first set's over."

"I reckon," Johnny said.

He walked out into the late afternoon sunlight,

wondering what Frolich had wanted to ask. He turned toward the barbershop, planning to get a shave and bath, when he heard someone call, "Johnny." He looked back to see Sherm Balder standing in front of the courthouse motioning toward him as he shouted: "Come here. I want to talk to you."

—2—

At one time the courthouse had been the pride and joy of the old-timers like Sherm Balder and Frank Deere. The building, a two-story frame structure with the sheriff's office and jail on the ground floor, was a frame structure that had been painted white and had been the subject of some of Dakota Sam Weeks's most ecstatic paeans of praise when the homesteaders were moving in and there had been enough rain to raise a wheat crop.

The courthouse had not been painted for years. Now it had the weathered appearance of a molting Plymouth Rock rooster. The yard had grown up in weeds that no one had taken the trouble to cut and had become a fire hazard. The steps were spur scarred and worn down around the nails and two of the boards were broken.

As Johnny crossed the street and strode up the walk, he thought that the courthouse was symbolic of the decay and apathy that was so characteristic of the town and the country around it. He followed Sherm Balder into his office and sat down on one of the cane-bottom chairs, the stink from the jail that was next to the office coming to him. He had often thought that being locked up even for one night in the jail would be as close to hell as man would ever be in his mortal life.

Sherm Balder sat down at his rolltop desk and filled his pipe, his weathered face showing more worry than Johnny had ever seen in it before. He was an old man in the way he talked and looked and moved. So was Johnny's father, although both were barely sixty, but the funny thing was that neither was ever called old, but Bull Tatum was.

Obviously it was one of those queer quirks of human nature that had no explanation, perhaps like calling the barber, Mike Malone, Curly when his head had no more hair than a steer's horn. Johnny put it out of his mind and fidgeted in his chair as he watched Sherm slowly tamp the tobacco into the bowl of his pipe.

"I figured to get a shave and a bath," Johnny said. "Maybe I'd better tell Curly to heat some water."

Sherm looked up. "You figuring to go to the dance?"

Johnny nodded. "That's what I rode into town for. I'm taking Linda."

Sherm very carefully placed his pipe on top of his desk and rose. He walked around the desk, keeping his hand on it as long as he could, then he moved slowly across the room to the hall door and a moment later Johnny heard him yell at the hotel man, Harlan Spain, "Tell Curly to heat some water. Johnny's coming over for a shave and a bath soon."

Spain had been sitting on a bench in front of the hotel whittling when Johnny had left the livery stable. He probably was still there. Johnny rolled and lighted a cigarette, watching Sherm return to his desk, walking in that slow, old-man way. He eased down into his chair and struck a match. He held the flame to his pipe, but his hand trembled so much he had trouble firing the tobacco.

When he finally had it going, he said between puffs, "Don't do it, Johnny."

"Don't do what?"

"Don't take Linda to the dance."

"What the hell, Sherm!" Johnny leaned forward, staring at the sheriff. "It's my business who I take to the dance."

"No." Sherm shook his head. "Not when the girl is Linda Hollison. That makes it more'n a date. It becomes everybody's business. I'm supposed to keep the peace, but if you take that girl to the dance, I can't. I won't even try."

Johnny got up and with a sudden, violent gesture threw his cigarette into the spittoon beside the desk. "My God, Sherm," he said hotly, "are you trying to tell me that things are so rotten in this county that the sheriff has to tell a man who he can or can't take to a dance?"

Sherm rose and walked to the window and stared at the weed-covered yard. His shoulders were slumped, his motions those of a very tired old man. He said: "That sounds pretty bad, putting it the way you do, but it's the truth. You see, Tom and Linda had a big row last Sunday. I ain't sure what it was all about, but part of it was on account of Tom wants to get married right away, and Linda, she ain't ready to get married, and accused Tom of wanting her to move out to Rainbow just to be a cheap housekeeper."

"It's probably true."

Sherm nodded. "That may be, but it don't make no never mind if it is. Tom looked me up Sunday evening, so mad he couldn't talk straight. He'd stopped at the hotel bar and had a few drinks. Anyhow, drunk or sober, he made it plenty plain. He said I was to see that you or nobody else took Linda anywhere. It was gonna be him or nobody. Well, it was a purty sure bet that you're the only one who's got the guts to buck Tom Tatum. O' course you've been playing tag with fire for quite a spell, stopping at Linda's house on a Saturday afternoon and kissing her and her fighting you off but not wanting to stop you real bad."

He turned from the window and made a weary

motion with his right hand. "Maybe you like kissing Linda, but you never took her nowhere and you have taken every other girl in the country to dances and basket socials and such. It seems purty plain to me that what you're really trying to do is to hooraw Tom. That's the way it strikes him, too, and he says he's going to put a stop to it."

Johnny grinned. "I hope he tries."

Sherm walked back to his desk and eased down into his chair. He said: "I know you ain't afraid of Tom, but don't tell me you ain't afraid of old Bull. I am and so's your pa and so's everybody else."

"Sure I am," Johnny said defiantly, "but I ain't going to get down on my knees and suck his behind. That's what's the matter with the whole country."

"I know, I know," Sherm said sadly, "but I don't figure we're any different than other towns and counties. They all have a big man who gives the orders. It happens in the cities, too. They've got their bosses same as we do. Sometimes they use force or money, or maybe they manipulate the law. Old Bull uses all three methods. You know what'll happen if you take the girl. She don't mean nothing to you, so why be a fool?"

Johnny jammed his hands into his pockets, the recklessness throbbing in his head like a pulse beat. He remembered what his father had said, not to get into trouble he couldn't get out of. He said: "Sherm, this country has been going to hell in a basket, and all because you and Pa and everyone let old Bull run roughshod over everybody. There was a time when you could have trimmed him down. Maybe it's too late now, but I aim to give it a whirl."

"But you don't mean nothing to Linda," Sherm protested, "and she don't mean nothing to you."

"That's right," Johnny said, "which same has got nothing to do with it."

Johnny wheeled and strode out of the office, leaving Sherm Balder sitting at his desk and staring moodily after him. He took a deep breath when he was outside, wondering if he would ever get the stink of the jail out of his nostrils. He wasn't sure what it was, probably a combination of sweaty bodies and vomit and urine, and the disinfectant Sherm used in a half-hearted way which didn't help at all.

Maybe, too, he thought as he strode angrily across the street to the barbershop, that people who allowed their lives to rot under the blight of old Bull Tatum's power had a stench of their own. Perhaps that was what he had smelled and it was the reason he still smelled it now that he was out here on the street.

As he walked past the hotel, he nodded at Harlan Spain who was chewing tobacco and whittling on a pine stick, and smiled when he wondered what Sherm would have said if he had told him what might have caused the smell.

He stepped into the barbershop and hung his dusty

Stetson on a nail in the wall. Curly Mike Malone was stropping his razor in an effort to appear busy. Johnny said in a grave tone, "Howdy, Curly. My bawth ready?"

"Howdy, Johnny," Curly said in an equally grave tone. "Your bawth will not be ready until I shave that growth of cactus off your face."

Johnny sat down in the chair and leaned back, his eyes closed. "Curly, business sure must be slow, with you having to blackmail a man into getting a shave."

The barber sighed. "Slower'n a barrel of molasses running into Pole Creek on Christmas. My wife and kids ain't et real good all summer except for the garden sass they get out of the backyard. I'm behind on my rent money to Sherm, too."

Johnny was silent then, relaxing under Malone's ministering hands and the hot towel and lather and the strokes of the sharp razor and finally feeling the sting and smelling the good, rich aroma of bay rum.

Malone jerked the apron away with a professional flourish as he said: "I reckon the water's hot. Help yourself."

"I'll do that." Johnny glanced down at his shirt, aware of the ground-in dirt. "Have you got time to go over to the Mercantile and pick up a clean shirt for me? I want to get into the tub and I sure can't go to the dance in this."

Malone twisted the point of his sweeping white

mustache as he frowned thoughtfully, then he added with facetious gravity, "Son, you sure want a lot of service for four bits."

"Cash money," Johnny said. "Besides, you can afford to give service to a brave man like me. Tonight I make a strike for liberty and freedom."

Malone's face turned barren, the good humor leaving it. "Then you are taking Linda to the dance?"

"You bet."

"I'll go get your shirt," Malone said, "but you ain't what I call a brave man. You're just a plain idiot, and if Sherm Balder wasn't a bigger idiot, he'd throw you into jail and keep you there till after the dance was over."

Malone stalked out. Johnny went into the back room and poured the kettles of steaming water into the zinc tub, then filled a bucket several times from the pump and cooled the bath water until it was comfortably warm.

He set the half-filled bucket on the floor beside the tub, undressed and, stepping into the water, lay back and closed his eyes. At least Malone hadn't lectured him the way Sherm Balder had, but Sherm had been right on one point as much as Johnny hated to admit it. Taking Linda to the dance was more than a date. It had become a community problem.

J ohnny did not hear the door open and did not know anyone had come into the room until the half bucket of cold water splashed over his head. He let out a howl, pawed the water out of his eyes, and opened them to see his friend Dan Foley standing there laughing so hard he couldn't say a word.

Johnny lunged out of the tub and pounded Foley on the back with his wet hands, shouting, "You son of a bitch, why didn't you tell me I was gonna get a shower?"

Foley pounded Johnny in return. As soon as he found his voice, he said, "Son, I just couldn't turn down the temptation. I opened the door and I seen you lying there with your eyes shut, soaking up that hot water and dreaming about a passel of purty girls, then I seen the water and I tell you I couldn't help myself."

Johnny picked up a towel and started to dry. "I notice you opened that door mighty quiet. Looks to me like you was up to some devilment all the time."

"I wasn't fixing to turn down opportunity if it showed its ugly head," Foley admitted. "It's too hot to think up something good, like carrying Curly's privy in and dropping it into the tub." He started to laugh again. "Remember the Halloween when we shoved Doc Allen's privy up against his back door and nailed his front door shut and he poked his head out of his bedroom window yelling for the sheriff? I'll never forget how the old booger looked with that nightcap he was wearing dangling across his face and he was slapping at it like he was fighting mosquitoes."

"I remember, all right." Johnny didn't laugh. It didn't seem very funny now. "I remember Sherm got there faster'n we figured he could and I took a load of salt in my butt from his shotgun and you got off scot free."

"That's me," Foley said. "I always get off scot free."

"Not this time. Go fetch my shirt. I told Curly to get me a new one from the Mercantile."

"Well now, who was your servant this time last year?"

"You were if I could get you to do anything which ain't never real easy."

Foley grunted and disappeared into the barbershop. Johnny grinned as he thought about him. Dan Foley was two years older measured by time and about five years younger measured by behavior. Johnny doubted if Foley would ever grow up. In some ways he envied the man. At least he never worried about old Bull Tatum's domineering habits or the town's decay or Sherm Balder's and his father's shattered dreams.

In fact, Dan Foley never worried about anything as far as Johnny knew. He was the youngest of a family of boys who worked the Rafter F with their father, old Rip Foley, a good-sized spread five miles up the creek from town. He had been Johnny's best friend from the time they had started grade school together and he still was. In fact, he was about the only friend Johnny had because the other fellows his age had drifted out of the country or were riding for old Bull Tatum's Rainbow which automatically lifted them to a higher social level and made them arrogantly contemptuous of boys who had been their friends.

Foley returned with the shirt and tossed it to Johnny who had put on his undershirt and drawers. Foley said, "Hurry it up, son. My gut's so empty it's growling and slapping against my backbone. We just got back from taking a jag of steers to Julesburg and I got paid, so I'll buy your supper."

"I sure won't turn that down," Johnny said. "I wish there was a lawyer in town, though. I'd feel better if we got it down in black and white."

"Got what down?" Foley asked suspiciously.

"The agreement. A contract. A simple legal document stating that you, John Doe Foley, agrees to buy a supper for me, Richard Roe Deere, and promises to wash dishes to pay for said supper if he's broke which I figure he is."

"Oh hell, I ain't broke." Foley flipped a silver dollar into the air and caught it. "See? I'm rich."

Johnny finished dressing and buckled his gun belt

around his waist. "All set," he said, and followed Foley through the barbershop into the street, Mike Malone ignoring them.

When they were outside, Foley asked, "What's the matter with old curly top? He acts like maybe he thinks we're Typhoid Mary's."

"He's sore because I'm taking Linda to the dance."

Foley stopped, his big right hand dropping to Johnny's shoulder. "You're what?"

"You heard me."

"I heard something, but then I figured maybe it was just the wind blowing." Foley's fingers squeezed Johnny's shoulder. "I don't believe what I thought I heard. Say it over."

"I am taking Linda Hollison to the dance," Johnny said. "If Tom Tatum shows up and gets ornery, I'll separate him from some teeth."

"All right, I'll believe it now that I'm sure you said it." Foley dropped his hand to his side and they walked on to the hotel lobby and strode through it to the dining room. They sat down at a table and Foley picked up a fly-specked menu, then put it down. "By God, I don't believe it now that I think about it. You used to be a little smart. Not much, but a little. Now if you really are taking Linda, I guess you've lost all the brain you ever had."

It was the first time in the years Johnny had known Foley that he could remember seeing a worried frown on the man's usually placid face. "All right," Johnny said. "I'm not smart." He tapped the menu. "I suppose you want me to order ham and beans 'cause it's only two bits, but I'm gonna have a steak a foot long and then I'll cover it with ketchup an inch thick."

"Sure, sure," Foley said. "Now you listen to me, son. Stopping and talking to Linda on a Saturday afternoon and kissing her once in a while is one thing. Maybe it's a good thing. It's fun and it gives the old women something to gab about and Tom something to bawl Linda out about, but taking her to a dance is different. Tom will ride in with the whole Rainbow outfit and they'll shoot the town up and fill you full of holes."

"No they won't," Johnny said. "He'll come alone 'cause this is between him and me, and I'll clean his plow for him."

Doc Allen's girl Myrtle came out of the kitchen to take their order. She said, "I hear you're taking Linda to the dance, Johnny?"

"What if I am?"

"My, my, ain't you the proddy one?" Myrtle giggled. "Why, I was just thinking Linda was lucky, seeing as you and Dan are the only single fellows around except for old bachelors and widowers and such, and with Tom Tatum being too big and important to come to a dance in Star City." She looked at Foley. "Who are you taking, Dan?"

"You, looks like," Foley said. "You ain't the best

dancer or the prettiest girl in town, but you've got the most cheek."

"Sure I have." She slapped him on the back. "You won't regret it, Mr. Foley. Not one bit."

"Now go fetch us a steak," Foley said. "Tell Mrs. Hollison who it's for. She knows how to cook for us."

"She sure does and so do I," Myrtle said. "I'll run the steer through the dining room and cut off a steak from the hind quarter as he goes past. Chances are you'll have to slap it back into your plate when I bring it to you or it'll walk across the room."

Myrtle walked back to the kitchen, giggling as if she thought what she'd said was excruciatingly funny. Foley watched her until the door slapped shut, his eyes frankly speculative. "You know, when Ma empties a jelly glass and sets it on the table, it quivers just like Myrtle's hind end does. How about it, Johnny? You've had Myrtle down by the river."

"Don't do it," Johnny said. "You won't sleep for a month afterwards wondering about her."

"Yeah, I guess that's right," Foley shuddered. "I wish I hadn't ordered a steak. I won't be able to eat it."

"Why not?"

"Just thinking about having to live with Myrtle the rest of my life," Foley said, "is enough to tie my stomach up into knots. I won't be able to choke anything down."

But he did. Johnny was the one who had to quit

before he finished his steak. He started thinking about what he'd told Sherm Balder, that Linda didn't mean anything to him. He had no idea why he'd said it. She meant a great deal to him. She was the most exciting girl he had ever met, and he knew he'd marry her tonight if she'd have him. He'd take her to the ranch to live if she'd go, and that, he thought, would be about the worst thing he could do to her.

Johnny and his father lived in a sod house. It had a dirt floor and a dirt roof with grass and flowers and prickly pear growing out of it, and the roof leaked every time it rained. The worst part of it was that no matter if you worked your tail off morning, noon, and night you'd never under God's sun make more than a bare living off the ranch. He couldn't do it, he told himself.

When Myrtle brought their pie, she said, "Johnny, Mrs. Hollison wants to see you before you go."

He looked at the girl, his temper soaring. "I don't want to see her," he said. "I've had people telling me all afternoon not to take Linda to the dance and I'm sick and tired of it."

Myrtle wasn't giggling now. She moistened her lips with the tip of her tongue, frowning, then she said, "I don't think it's that, Johnny. You'd better see her."

"All right," he said. "I'll go back into the kitchen before I go."

After Myrtle left, Foley said, "Wonder what she wants."

"Dunno," Johnny said.

He ate his pie and rose. Foley said, "Go get the message Mrs. Hollison wants to whisper in your little pink ear and come back. I'll help you fetch Linda to the dance."

"The hell you will," Johnny said. "You tend to Myrtle and I'll take care of Linda and thanks for the supper."

Several other men had come into the dining room. When Johnny pushed the swinging door back, he saw that Mrs. Hollison was bending over the stove. She glanced around and saw him, then said something to Myrtle about watching the steak and jerked her head toward the door that opened into the alley.

Mrs. Hollison was in her middle thirties. Johnny had heard the story about her often enough. She had married a drummer when she was sixteen and had left town with him to live in Denver, but six months later she was back. Her husband had deserted her for another woman and she returned to have her baby.

She stayed with her folks, and when they died several months later, they left her the house where she and Linda lived. She went to work for Harlan Spain, and if she ever felt that life had been unfair to her, she never admitted it to anyone. Now she was a slender, gracious woman, straight-backed and pretty, but as far as Johnny knew, she had nothing to do with any of the single men who continually pestered her with offers of marriage.

Johnny stood in front of her, waiting. The sun was down, the twilight rapidly becoming darkness. Mrs. Hollison wiped her face with a corner of her apron and said, "It's nice to get out of that kitchen for a minute and catch a breath of fresh air."

She swallowed and tipped her head back to look at him. She said: "Johnny, this is hard for me to say. I love Linda. She's all I have and I want her to be happy, but she won't be because she's never satisfied with what she has. I won't ask you to not take Linda to the dance, but if you do, keep your eyes open. I know what Linda does to men. She knows, too. I guess she . . . she enjoys it."

She paused, and he said, "Yes, ma'am."

"All I want to say is that she's using you to get at Tom Tatum. They had a quarrel Sunday. She wanted him to do some things before they were married. I'm not one to pry and she didn't tell me all about it, but she did mention that she wanted a house for her and Tom to live in so they wouldn't have to move into the big house with Tom's father. But it isn't important what they quarreled about. The important thing is that she's using you to make Tom jealous so she can get him to do what she wants."

Mrs. Hollison paused, her eyes on Johnny. He stood in front of her, straight and very stiff, not sure if she was finished. She asked, "You believe me, don't you, Johnny?"

"No, ma'am," he said, and walked past her and went down the alley toward the Hollison house.

— 4 —

Johnny found the front door of Linda's house open. A hobnail lamp on the claw-footed stand in the middle of the front room was lighted. Johnny, standing in the doorway, saw that the room was empty. Then he remembered that her bedroom was upstairs and he was a few minutes early.

He knocked, and Linda called from her room, "That you, Johnny?"

"It's me."

"Come in. I'll be down in a minute."

He went into the front room, glancing at the meager furniture. Besides the stand, there was a black leather couch set against one wall, two rocking chairs with headrests made of ribbons of various colors, and three cane-bottom chairs. A picture on the wall showed a little girl running toward a cliff, her guardian angel hovering above her with a hand outstretched. Across from it on the opposite wall was a framed piece of needlework with the letters, GOD BLESS OUR HOME.

That was all. Comfortable and clean, but very simple. Mrs. Hollison made enough working for Harlan Spain to pay the taxes and buy their groceries and clothes. That was all. Linda worked occasionally, taking Myrtle Allen's place in the hotel dining room when Myrtle was sick or when she took a trip to Denver which she did about every three months. Now and then Linda gave Pete Goken a hand in the Mercantile at Christmas or when the regular clerk was sick, but she spent everything she made on her clothes and so was no help as far as taking care of the house expenses were concerned.

Johnny sat down on the leather couch and rolled a smoke, but he didn't light it. He held it in his hand and stared at it. Mrs. Hollison's words beat against his ears; "I know what Linda does to men. She knows, too. I guess she enjoys it." And, "She's using you to make Tom jealous so she can get him to do what she wants."

He crumpled the cigarette in his hand. He knew Linda was a flirt. He'd seen her perform often enough. He remembered her saying this afternoon that he'd have a fight on his hands and she'd be the cause of it. Well, she'd been the cause of plenty of fights even when she'd been in school.

But he couldn't believe she had lied to him this afternoon. She'd said she wanted him to be her fellow, but she'd been honest. She'd told him not to take her, that they'd kill him. After that she'd said she wouldn't throw him away when she was done with him. He shut his eyes and shook his head, his hands clenched so tightly that the nails bit into his palms.

He had been in love with her for a long time. He'd told himself that he didn't have any chance, with her engaged to Tom Tatum and Tom having more money than anybody else in the county. But this afternoon she'd made it plain enough that he had every chance in the world. He'd be the worst kind of fool if he didn't believe her. Mrs. Hollison must be mistaken.

"Johnny."

He hadn't heard her on the stairs. He jumped at the sound of her voice and opened his eyes. He stood up and took a long breath, his fists opening, the wadded-up cigarette dropping to the floor. She was wearing a blue dress with ruching around the neck, her waist unbelievably small, her breasts firm and pointed under her bodice. She wore an aigrette in her hair, with gay, jeweled combs on both sides of her head.

"Honey, you're just standing there staring at me," she complained. "Don't you like me?"

"Like you?" he asked softly. "You bet I like you. You're Aphrodite or some of them other goddesses that the Greeks worshipped. When I was reading about them in the eighth grade, I never knew I'd see one sometime."

"Johnny, you are so crazy," she said, laughing softly. "Are you ready?"

He walked to her slowly, tempted to tell her that everyone in town had warned him about taking her to the dance and even her own mother had said to keep his eyes open, that she was just using him. But when he took her hands and looked down at her, he knew he couldn't say it. He might as well come right out and tell her he didn't trust her, and you couldn't do that with a girl you loved and hoped to marry.

"Linda," he said, "I know you've been flirting with me and I never took you seriously because I figured you and Tom would get married. But I love you anyhow. I haven't got anything to offer you except a sod house that you can't keep clean, and hard work on a ranch that never will make us rich. I'm asking you to marry me anyhow. I won't push you for an answer tonight, but later . . . maybe next Saturday you can tell me after you think it over."

"Johnny honey, of course I love you," she said. "You never have taken me seriously and that's a fact. I used to cry myself to sleep trying to think of something I could do to let you know how much I thought of you."

He brought her to him and kissed her, and it was the same as it had been in the afternoon except that the flame burned higher in her and so kindled a greater fire in him. Whatever had possessed him to tell Sherm Balder she meant nothing to him was something he would never know. She was everything. He turned her toward the couch, half crazy with his hunger for her, but she slipped out of his arms, laughing gaily.

"Not here and not now, Johnny honey," she said,

"with Mamma about to come through the front door any minute."

He wiped a hand across his face, suddenly ashamed. "I'm sorry, Linda. You don't know what you do to a man when you kiss him. I didn't intend . . ."

He floundered and stopped, and she laughed again. "Johnny Deere, I know exactly what you intended and I'm not shocked a bit. It makes me feel good to make a man want me. I want you, too, but I know what's right and what isn't. I'm not Myrtle Allen, Johnny. You'd better know that right now."

"I do," he said. "I told you I'm sorry."

"Well then," she said, "I'll blow out the lamp and we'll go to the dance."

She held his hand, her lavender perfume a heady scent that kept his blood throbbing in his temples. Her mother had to be wrong, he told himself. She just had to be.

She blew out the lamp and they felt their way through the darkness to the front porch. She closed the door and they walked along the boardwalk to the street.

They were halfway to the Oddfellows Hall over Gokens Mercantile when she said, "I suppose Mamma warned you about me."

"Why, yes she did," he said, surprised. "How did you know?"

She laughed as if it were a joke. "Well, you see,

Mamma said she was going to if she had a chance. You know, Johnny, sometimes I think she doesn't approve of her daughter. Don't misunderstand me. I love her, but a girl like me gets talked about and Mamma acts as if she believes everything she hears in the hotel. She's with Myrtle all the time and Myrtle's a . . . a . . ."

"I know what she is," Johnny said.

They reached the outside stairs that led to the Odd-fellows Hall, and paused to let a young couple named Quinn, who lived in the sand hills south of the Deere place, go on ahead of them. The man carried a cake in one hand and a baby in the other. His wife had a second, smaller child in a clothes basket. Johnny knew them well, for he and his father exchanged work with Benny Quinn occasionally.

He drew Linda back until the Quinns had disappeared at the top of the stairs. He said, "Linda, they live on a little spread about like ours and they'll never make any more off it than they're making right now no matter how hard they work. It's a tough life on both of them."

"I know, Johnny," she said in a low voice, "and with two babies in less than a year. But there are other places to live and other kinds of work. We'll make out all right."

"Sure," he said, relieved. "You bet we will."

They went up the stairs together. He felt as if he

were ten feet tall. He hadn't pressed her for an answer, but it was plain enough she would say yes, maybe tonight when he took her home.

Dan Foley stood just inside the door. When Johnny came in with Linda, Foley let out a whoop and gave Johnny a great thump on the back. "So you did fetch the prettiest girl on Pole Creek. How'd you manage it, you old fox?"

Linda laughed as if pleased. "The prettiest girl, you say?"

"Sure you are." Foley motioned toward the floor. The first dance had just started and Myrtle Allen went by in Pete Goken's arms. "Don't tell Myrtle what I said. I brung her." He raised his big hand to his mouth and whispered, "Myrtle ain't purty and she can't dance worth a doggone, but she's sure a lot of woman."

Linda slapped him lightly and laughed. "Be careful you don't get your women mixed up, Mr. Foley." She tugged at Johnny's arm. "We're wasting time, honey?"

"Honey is it now?" Foley said as if surprised. "What's going on, Johnny? A big surprise coming maybe?"

"Maybe," Johnny said, grinning and still feeling ten feet tall.

"Wait, son," Foley said. "I forgot. No guns. You leave 'em at the door. Sherm's orders. That's why I'm here and why that doggone Pete Goken is dancing with Myrtle. Sherm stepped out and it's time he was back here doing his own job."

Johnny hesitated, questioning eyes on Foley, then he began to unbuckle the gun belt. Before he finished, Harlan Spain came up and swept Linda onto the dance floor.

"Now you done it," Johnny said. "You made me miss the first dance with Linda."

"Old Harlan ain't young enough to do nothing." Foley took the gun belt from Johnny's hand and hung it on the wall. "It's different with Pete and Myrtle. She's willing and able. If I don't watch 'em, they'll sneak out and then I'd have to kill Pete, wouldn't I?"

"She ain't worth it," Johnny said.

"No, she ain't for a fact," Foley admitted, his eyes on Linda and Spain. "But Linda now, she'd be worth it."

"You told me I'd lost the little bit of brain I had for fetching her," Johnny said.

Foley shrugged. "All depends on whether Tom and his crowd shows or not. If they don't, I reckon you're smart enough."

Johnny stood watching the dancers, feeling naked without his gun. If the Rainbow crew did come and Tom Tatum was pushing for a fight, Johnny Deere might wind up as stupid as Foley thought and very dead.

His eyes searched Linda out in the crowd of dancers. She smiled at him over Harlan Spain's shoulder and moved her lips to say something to him that might have been, "I love you." He hoped that's what it was. Right then he was more than ten feet tall. Let the whole Rainbow outfit come. He'd take them on single-handed and he'd show Dan Foley how stupid he was.

He relaxed then and waited until the dance was finished. It was wild and breathless, and he wondered how the women who had worked hard all week could come here Saturday night and be swung and whirled for hours by bronze-skinned men in shirt sleeves who danced as if the end of the world was at hand and this was the last dance they would have short of eternity.

It would go on this way until close to midnight when it would be time to eat. The tables at the far end of the long room were heaped with cakes and pies and sandwiches. Before long Harlan Spain would leave and brew huge pots of coffee in the hotel kitchen and bring them to the hall. Everyone would stop dancing long enough to consume the mountain of food and gallons of coffee and then go right back to it again.

The Quinns and the other couples like them would not get home until after daylight. Both of their babies were asleep in the clothes basket under the tables in line with a dozen more. The dances were the only entertainment these people had, and they would look forward to the next one sometime in September. Unless they were sick, they would all be here.

When the set was finished, Linda came directly to Johnny and, slipping her arm through his, hugged it. "I'm sorry," she said contritely. "I know you should have had the first dance, but Dan was holding you up and Harlan came along and dragged me off." She hesitated, and then added, "Johnny, it's just that Mamma works for him and sometimes he thinks that gives him a special claim on me, I guess."

"I don't mind," he said. "Looks like Dakota Sam's about to wind up again. I'm not letting you get away from me this time."

She looked at him, smiling, her lips parted, and it seemed to him she was letting him know she loved him and was going to be happy and she wanted everyone in the hall to see and know. Then Dakota Sam Weeks yelled, "Let her go," and began tapping his foot as he pulled the bow of his fiddle across the strings.

Linda was a feather in Johnny's arms, a wonderful feather of flesh and bone and passion, and he could think of nothing except that she loved him. It was the greatest knowledge that had ever entered his consciousness. Suddenly Dakota Sam stopped playing, the last sound an awful catlike howl.

From the door Dan Foley shouted: "Look out, Johnny. He's here."

Couples rushed toward the sides of the room. He felt Linda stiffen and pull away from him, then she, too, ran to the side where the Quinns stood. Alone now in the middle of the room, he made a slow turn toward the door, knowing what he would see. Tom Tatum stood thirty feet away, staring at him, his face dark with the fury that possessed him.

Johnny waited, spread-legged, motionless. Silence then until one of the babies woke and started to cry, a wailing sound that seemed inordinately loud in the breathless silence. Johnny, his gaze locked with Tatum's, noted two facts which surprised him. The man was alone, and he was not wearing a gun.

— 5 —

Tom Tatum was a big, heavy-featured man, not as tall as Johnny, but thicker in the shoulders and arms. Johnny had never understood how Linda could stand him. He was arrogant in a peevish sort of way. To Johnny it was a phony arrogance, probably assumed because he was old Bull Tatum's son and so knew it was expected of him. Now, meeting his gaze, Johnny realized he was out of his head, turned crazy by jealousy or rage or both.

Tatum started pacing toward Johnny, moving in the jerky manner of a marionette being led across a stage. His big hands hung at his sides, his fingers moving convulsively. He said, slurring his words the way a drunk would do, "I'm going to kill you, Deere." Suddenly Johnny realized his eyes were feverish with the look of a man who was running a high temperature.

Johnny shot a glance at the men by the door. Sherm Balder was standing beside Dan Foley. Pete Goken and Curly Mike Malone were close enough to grab Johnny's gun off the wall, but none of them moved. They were watching as if they were hypnotized.

Johnny had time to take a quick look at Linda who had backed up to stand beside Benny Quinn. She was smiling, a strange, feline smile that he had never seen on her face before, and he remembered her saying, "Either way, first or last, you'll have a fight on your hands and I'll be the cause of it."

Johnny, puzzled and a little sick, brought his eyes back to Tatum just as he pulled a knife from under his belt and lunged forward, the long steel blade shiny bright in the lamplight as it slashed at him.

Johnny swung to one side and the blade flashed by. Tatum, carried forward by the momentum of his lunge, stumbled and Johnny drove a fist to the side of his head. He went down, falling hard, the floor shaking under his weight. He got up to his hands and knees, the knife still clutched in his right hand, and stared at Johnny, his chin trembling.

"You've got no fight with me, Tom," Johnny said. "Get out of here. They'll hang you if you kill me."

Spit drooled from both sides of his mouth and dripped to the floor. He said again, still slurring his words, "I'm going to kill you, Deere."

He didn't move for a time, and Johnny wondered why the men at the door didn't stop it, and why Tom Tatum was so fanatically determined to destroy him. Had old Bull pushed him into it, or was it Linda's needling last Sunday? And most of all, why was Linda smiling? What was there to smile about when two men who were in love with her were fighting over her?

Johnny had the distorted feeling that this scene was frozen, with no one talking and no one moving, and that time ran on and on. There was no sound except his labored breathing and Tom Tatum's panting. But it was an illusion; he knew that Tatum was not on the floor for more than a few seconds, then he was up again and lunging forward, the knife sweeping out in another wild swing that would have disemboweled Johnny if the steel had found its mark.

Again Johnny dodged and swung his fist, but this time he failed to land a solid blow. Tatum's left arm circled Johnny's waist and clung there as he swung half around, turning Johnny with him so that for a moment it seemed as if they were dancing partners.

For a time they stumbled across the room together, Tatum clinging desperately to Johnny and Johnny trying just as desperately to hit him and knock him loose, but he did little more than paw at Tatum because he was carried by the man's momentum, never quite succeeding in regaining his balance so he could put any real power into a blow.

Then they crashed to the floor, Johnny on top. He heard the solid *thwack* of Tatum's head against the boards, then a strange hissing noise that sounded like air escaping from a balloon. When he regained his feet, he looked down and saw that Tatum was lying on his stomach, motionless.

The fall had knocked him out, or at least had taken the fight out of him. Johnny said, "Ready to quit, Tom?"

Tatum did not move and did not say anything. Johnny reached down and, catching him by a shoulder, turned him over on his back. For a moment Johnny couldn't breathe, his heart beating in great sledging blows. The knife had gone into Tom Tatum's chest the entire length of the blade so that now only the horn handle was visible. Blood bubbled from his mouth and ran down his chin.

A woman screamed. A strange sigh rose from the crowd as if the spectators were exhausted, then Linda was flying across the room. Johnny turned to catch her but she flung herself to the floor and lifted Tatum's head to her lap.

"You can't die, Tom," she cried. "Please don't die. I never intended for it to happen. Not like this."

Johnny stared at her, dazed. This couldn't be Linda Hollison who less than an hour ago was talking about loving him, not Tom Tatum, and about living somewhere else than in the sand hills and assuring him they would make out all right.

Sherm Balder said to Harlan Spain, "Go get her ma." Spain nodded and left the hall a few steps behind Benny Quinn. A little later the sound of hoofbeats receded down the street, and Sherm muttered, "I reckon Benny will make a dollar, taking the word to old Bull."

And Dan Foley said, "We'd best get Johnny out of here."

Some of the crowd had moved forward to stand around Johnny who was still staring at the top of Linda's head. She was crooning over Tatum, saying she never intended it to happen, that she would have married him all the time.

"Linda," Johnny said.

She didn't hear him. He thought desperately that this must be a nightmare, that he'd started dreaming this afternoon when she'd talked about wanting him for her fellow and had said she would go to the dance with him, and he'd kept on dreaming tonight when she'd talked about crying herself to sleep because she couldn't think of a way to let him know how much she thought of him.

But it wasn't a nightmare. Sherm Balder was tugging at an arm and saying: "Johnny, come over to the office with me. I've got to talk to you."

Johnny shook his hand off and knelt beside Linda. He said, "You love me. Remember? We talked about it when we were coming to the dance."

She had laid her cheek against Tatum's and some of his blood made a red smear along the side of her face. Apparently she hadn't heard what he'd said. She stared at him, her eyes wide and wild, and she screamed, "You murdered Tom. Arrest him, Sheriff. Take him out and hang him."

Sherm dropped his hand to Johnny's shoulder. "Come on, boy. You've got to get out of here."

Johnny ignored him. He said, "I love you, Linda, and you love me. Don't you remember all the things we said?"

She spat at him. "Love you?" she cried. "Oh, what a fool you are! What a stupid fool! I wouldn't have been seen with you tonight if I hadn't wanted to make Tom jealous. Mamma was right about me, but you were too much of an idiot to believe her. You think I'd go out to the pigpen where you live and move in with you and that . . . that dirty old man who's your father?"

Johnny got up and wiped the spit from his face. This was a nightmare, all right. It had to be. He stared at Linda who was crooning over Tatum again, this time saying something about she'd live in the big house with him and his father if that was what they wanted.

Now Sherm Balder had hold of one of Johnny's arms. Dan Foley caught the other. Sherm said, "Come on, Johnny. This is no place for you."

"I didn't murder him." Johnny knew his lips were moving, but it must have been someone else's voice, someone a long ways off. "He came at me with a knife. It was an accident. We fell. You saw it."

"Yes, it was an accident," Sherm said.

They dragged him toward the door, the crowd opening in front of him, curious eyes staring at him. Someone, Johnny never knew who it was, said: "He was warned enough times about bringing that bitch to the dance, but he was too smart to listen. Now he'll pay for it."

Pay for what? He didn't know. He tried to break free from Sherm Balder's and Dan Foley's grip. He said, "I can walk. Let go."

"No," Sherm said. "I don't want you running off till I've talked to you. Curly, fetch his gun. It's that .45 yonder. The one on the far side."

"Damn it, let me go," Johnny yelled. "You got no call to drag me out of here like I was a murderer. You can't arrest me because Tom Tatum fell on his knife."

"I ain't arresting you," Sherm said, "but I'm taking you to my office and we're going to talk. Sure, I know it was an accident. So does everyone who saw it. Linda will know it, too, after she starts thinking."

He walked then, through the door and across the landing and down the stairs, Sherm holding one arm and Dan Foley the other. When they reached the street, Mrs. Hollison and Harlan Spain were coming on the run, Spain yelling, "Wait a minute, Sherm."

The sheriff said: "Hold up, Dan. What's wrong, Harlan?"

"Nothing," the hotel man said. "Mrs. Hollison wanted to speak to Johnny. That's all."

Mrs. Hollison put a hand on Johnny's arm. She said sadly, "I'm so sorry, Johnny. I was afraid this would happen. I tried to stop it but I couldn't. If you'd only believed what I told you."

He looked at her, his head aching with so much pain that he wasn't fully aware of what she had said. He wasn't sure for a moment who she was. The buildings across the street were tilting and whirling in front of him. If Sherm and Foley hadn't kept their hold on him, he would have pitched forward on his face. He felt as if he were coming out of a drugged sleep and couldn't quite return to life, couldn't make himself fully aware of what was happening to him.

Mrs. Hollison began to cry, then she wiped her eyes and turned to the sheriff. "I'm to blame for everything that's happened, Sherm. I've tried to raise Linda right, but it's been years since I was able to do anything with her. Or even talk to her."

"No, Mrs. Hollison," Dan Foley said. "It's not your fault. It's ours. Everybody's."

"Maybe yours, Dan," she said bitterly, "but it's mine, too. Not everybody's."

"It's everybody's," Sherm Balder said. "We could

have stopped it but we didn't. We've been afraid, so we just let it happen. Now it's too late."

"Johnny's a good boy," she said. "One of the best boys I've ever known. That's why Linda was able to use him. He trusted her and believed her, and he thought she really loved him. I know her, Sherm. I know how she thinks and what she will do to get what she wants. But it isn't right for Johnny to die. You've got to get him out of town."

"We will," Sherm said. "You'd best get upstairs to Linda. Doc Allen's up there. Maybe he can give her something to quiet her down."

Mrs. Hollison nodded and went up the stairs with Harlan Spain. Sherm Balder and Dan Foley continued on across the street with Johnny, Curly Mike Malone and Pete Goken coming behind. Johnny tried to make sense out of what Mrs. Hollison had said, tried to sort it out in his mind, but he couldn't think. The pressure in his head was too great.

Still, an uneasiness was in him and he wondered if something had happened that he had forgotten, something that made a criminal out of him. Mrs. Hollison had said it wasn't right for him to die, that he had to get out of town, but why? He didn't know. The answer must be in something that had been said back there at the foot of the stairs, but it eluded him. He was too furry-headed to think it through.

– 6 –

Johnny sat in Sherm Balder's office staring across the desk at the sheriff. He remembered being here this afternoon; he remembered the sickening stink from the jail and how Sherm had tried to talk him out of taking Linda to the dance.

That much was a clear-cut memory. He had been alone with Sherm then, but now Dave Foley, Pete Goken, and Curly Mike Malone were here. Then, as he sat trying to break through the mental fog that clouded his consciousness, Dakota Sam Weeks and Al Frolich came in.

Johnny was aware that Sherm had been saying something to him, something about "You've got to start riding now." He looked at Sherm who sat behind his desk and shook his head, remembering that Mrs. Hollison had said the same thing in her own words. It didn't make sense. Nothing was important except Linda. She said she didn't love him, but she did. He had to see her and remind her.

He rose. "I've got to find Linda," he said.

"Sit down," Sherm ordered. "Linda's sick. Doc Allen is with her. She can't see you."

"I didn't know she was sick," Johnny said, and sat down.

Sherm turned to Dan Foley. "I'm not getting any-

49

where with him," he said. "I don't know what else to say."

"Got a bottle here?" Foley asked.

Sherm nodded and, opening a desk drawer, lifted a bottle and a glass from it. Foley said, "Give him a drink. A good stiff one, then I'll talk to him."

The other men crowded forward, all of them tense and jumpy as they listened for the drum of hoofs. Sam Weeks said uneasily, "If old Bull's home, he'll be here anytime."

"I don't think he is," Al Frolich said. "He aimed to take most of his crew and ride over to the Frenchman to fetch back a herd of cows that a feller's got for sale over there. If he went, he won't get the word till tomorrow."

"Don't make no never mind," Curly Mike Malone said. "Jess Crowder's at Rainbow. He'll do what old Bull would do if he was home."

"That's right," Dan Foley said. "Al, go fetch Johnny's horse. Mine, too. I'll ride a ways with him. Pete, he's got to have some grub, enough to last him a few days. Fetch a .30-30 and some shells." He took off his hat and passed it to Malone. "He's likewise got to have some dinero. Dig down even if it hurts." He tossed a ten-dollar gold piece into his hat. "He ought to have enough to keep him eating till he gets a job."

"I'll fetch the Winchester and a box of shells," Goken said. "Some grub, too. I reckon that'll be my share."

"Sure, Pete." Foley turned to Johnny. "Son, I'm your friend. We've done about everything that two men could do together except sleep with the same woman. I wouldn't tell you anything that was wrong. You savvy that?"

Johnny gulped the drink. The whiskey jolted him and warmed him, and cut away some of the fog. He'd listened to the talk, but now he was silent for a time, unable to understand what was going on.

Foley said impatiently, "You savvy that I wouldn't give you a wrong steer?"

"Sure, Dan," Johnny said finally, "but why are you so anxious to get me out of town?"

"You killed Tom Tatum. Remember?"

"I remember, all right," Johnny said, anger stirring in him at the injustice of Foley's statement. "But I didn't kill him. It was an accident."

"Sure it was," Foley said, "but old Bull ain't gonna see it that way. Soon as he hears about it, he'll ride into town like he was clean loco. If you're here, he'll kill you and he won't wait to listen to how it happened. Old Bull will listen just long enough to hear that you and Tom had a fight and Tom got killed. Then he'll start hunting for you."

Johnny stood up and dropped a hand to his gun butt. "I never ran from anything or anybody, Dan," he said. "I ain't running from old Bull."

"It ain't just old Bull," Foley said, his impatience

growing. "He'll fetch Jess Crowder and the Rainbow crew and they'll hang you."

Johnny was thinking coherently enough and he was remembering, too, but now, his gaze moving from Sherm Balder, who was still sitting at his desk, on around the half circle of waiting men and back to Sherm, he sensed that there was something else he didn't understand, something he couldn't put his finger on. His head still throbbed. There must be something he couldn't remember.

"All right, old Bull rides into town with the Rainbow crew," he said slowly, "but he won't hang me. He won't fight all of us. You boys will side me. You're my friend, Dan. Remember?"

Dan Foley, who never took anything seriously and never worried about anything, frowned and backed up a step and shot a quick glance at Sherm. For once, Johnny thought, Foley was taking something seriously and he was worried.

"Sure I'm your friend, Johnny," Foley said, "and I'll do what I can for you, but even you don't have the right to ask me to commit suicide. Trying to fight Rainbow would be the same as shooting myself. If you ride out of town tonight and don't tell us where you're going, then old Bull can't get nothing out of us."

Johnny faced Sherm. "Arrest me for murder. Have me tried. There was fifty or more people in that hall tonight who saw what happened. I'd be acquitted and you know it."

"No, Johnny," Sherm said. "Think about it a minute. Do you believe that any of us have the guts it would take to tell the truth when we all know what old Bull would want us to say? You'd hang as sure as you're a foot high."

"All right then, don't arrest me," Johnny said. "If old Bull Tatum kills me, it will be murder. Arrest him and hang him."

Sherm drew in a long breath and let it out with a gusty sound. He said: "You're making us look at ourselves and it ain't a purty sight. You know I'd never arrest old Bull. If I did, he wouldn't be convicted."

"Ride out," Foley said. "It's the only way."

"You're spelling it out mighty plain, Johnny," Dakota Sam Weeks said hoarsely. "It's not a pretty sight when we look at ourselves and that's a fact, but we've been cowards from the day old Bull drove his herd up from Texas and threw it on the hard land north of Pole Creek. At the time I guess we didn't know where it was taking us, and we were all a little sick and scared because of the drought and the panic and the farmers moving out and all. The truth is we settled for something which was a little better than nothing, so we went out of our way to get along with old Bull. Now he's got us roped and tied."

"That's right," Curly Mike Malone said. "You've got to ride out."

Sherm nodded. "We are your friends, Johnny. Don't doubt that. We're telling you this because it's the best thing for all of us."

Johnny's lips curled in derision. His mind was working with sharp precision now. He understood exactly what was happening. He said, " 'Friend' is an empty word the way you use it, Sherm. You tried to talk me out of taking Linda because you were afraid of what old Bull would do to you, not to me, and you want me out of the country because you're afraid of what he will do to you when he finds out about Tom. Not one of you in this room gives a damn about me, so to hell with the bunch of you."

"We care, all right," Foley said. "If you weren't so muleheaded, you'd see it. I won't be hurt because I'm not a businessman, and me and my dad and brothers have always got along with the Tatums, but you ought to think about what will happen to Star City. Old Bull never cared anything about the town. Chances are he'll burn it out."

"Let him burn it," Johnny said. "Why shouldn't a town of cowards be burned?" He stared at Foley, wondering why the man was concerned. What he said was true. He wasn't involved the way the businessmen were. Then Johnny was aware that Al Frolich had come in.

"The horses are ready," Frolich said. "Pete's tying the grub back of Johnny's saddle."

"I'll ride with you, Johnny," Foley said. "If they come after us, I'll fight with you till they kill me, but if you stay here and put the town and everybody in it in danger, I won't raise a hand to keep 'em from hanging you."

"You'd better start thinking about your pa, too," Sherm said. "If you go home, old Bull will go out there and hang both of you. Frank has been my friend for a long time. I'd hate to see him hurt because of you."

Johnny sat down again. This was something he had not thought about. He reached for the bottle and poured a drink. He stared at it a moment, turning it with his fingers, then he raised the glass and drank, but he found no wisdom in the liquor. Whatever he did was wrong.

His father would be hurt if he rode out of the country. More than that, Johnny was needed to help with the work. But for the first time Sherm Balder had said something that had meaning. Old Bull would hang both of them, partly out of plain cussedness, but mostly because he could not afford to leave a witness.

Johnny was still staring at the empty glass when Doc Allen came in with Harlan Spain. Pete Goken had stepped into the room, too, so the sheriff's office was crowded. Foley asked, "How's Linda?"

"Sick," Allen said. "Sick in the head." He pushed forward and stopped beside Johnny. "Whatever you do, don't try to see her. She might kill you. She swears she will. I finally got her to take something before I left and I think she'll settle down, but she's been crazy wild. Her mother says she had her head set on marrying Tom Tatum because of his money, but she was trying to prove to him that he had to do what she said or she wouldn't marry him. Now she hates you because you killed the one man who could have made her a rich woman."

Johnny put a hand to his forehead. The throbbing had started again, but his mind wasn't fogged up the way it had been. He understood at last what Linda had tried to do and how she had used him, how she had lied to him and had never meant a word of it. All this time he had been excusing her, had tried to make himself believe that if he could talk to her, she would remember what she had said to him. Now he knew she had remembered, that her words and her kisses had had a purpose behind them.

He had been as big a fool as she had said he was and he knew then he did not want to stay here. He did not want to see her again; he did not want to see the people who had heard what she had said to him when he had knelt beside her and she had held Tom Tatum's head in her lap. He had been the worst kind of sucker, he had been humiliated, and he was ashamed in a deep, sickening way.

"I ain't real sure she'll ever be right again," Doc

Allen was saying. "Her ma says she can't give up any-thing once she sets her mind on it the way she was set on marrying Tom. I'm sorry mostly for Mrs. Hollison. Seems like she's had more than her share of trouble."

Johnny rose. "I'm riding out like you want, but it ain't because I give a damn about what happens to you bastards or this stinking town. It's a pimple on the bank of Pole Creek and it ought to be destroyed. I'm leaving for my own reasons." He leaned across the desk, his face close to Sherm Balder's. "If you ain't too big a coward, there's one thing I want you to do. Go out and tell Pa to make out the best he can. Tell him there's nothing to keep either one of us here. When I get settled, I'll send for him."

"I'll tell him," Sherm said.

"I'll ride a piece with you," Foley said.

"I can't stop you," Johnny said.

"Wait." Sherm had dropped the money they had collected into a buckskin bag and now pulled the drawstrings. "You might as well have it, Johnny. There's about fifty dollars. It'll keep you eating a while."

"Why not?" Johnny said, and, taking the bag, shoved it into his pocket and walked out.

He mounted and left town, headed west. Foley rode beside him. He tipped his head back and looked at the stars, and all the pain and misery that was in him boiled up and took hold of him. He raised his fist and shook it at the sky. "Damn you, God!" he shouted. "Why? Tell me why?"

But God didn't answer and neither did Dan Foley. Then the town was behind them, the lights lost to sight over a low ridge. After that there was no sound but the soft thud of hoofs dropping into the dust of the road.

−7−

Johnny and Dan Foley rode in silence until the sun was up. They had left the road hours ago to strike off across the short grass. Johnny had no plan, no destination, and he'd had no particular reason for leaving the road except that he had the vaguest of notions that he wanted to go to the mountains and the quickest way of reaching them was to ride straight west.

"I'm going back," Foley said. "If we had anybody on our tail, we'd have seen 'em afore now."

"Yeah," Johnny said, and stared straight ahead at the long swells of land ahead of them.

"What do you figure to do?"

"Dunno."

"Well, damn it," Foley said, "if you can't talk to me, who the hell can you talk to?"

"Dunno."

"You think I'm riding out here with you just because I like to feel a horse between my legs?" Foley demanded. "You think for a minute I'd have ridden fifty yards with you if I didn't care about what happened to you and didn't want to help you if you got into trouble?"

Johnny looked at the other man and was ashamed. Somehow this didn't seem to be the Dan Foley he had known since he was a boy, the Dan Foley who never had wanted anything but a good time, a joke, and a belly laugh.

"I'm sorry, Dan," Johnny said. "I guess you're the only living person except Pa who cares anything at all about what happens to me, and that's a sorry thing. Makes me wonder what I've done with all the twenty-one years of living I've used up."

"I know," Foley said bitterly. "I've had the same question nagging me for quite a spell. I'll tell you one thing, son. From now on it's gonna be different with me. There's more to living than getting drunk or taking some floozy like Myrtle Allen into the brush or cooking up a crazy, practical joke."

Foley was staring straight ahead now, frown lines digging deeply into his forehead. Johnny looked at him and wondered. He hadn't seen Foley for several weeks. Months even, because it was summer and they'd both been busy, but something had happened to the man. Johnny had begun to feel it when he'd told him he was taking Linda to the dance, a feeling that had steadily grown.

Thinking about what had happened in Sherm Balder's office, it struck Johnny that Foley had taken charge and that was something he had never known his friend to do before. He pondered this, not sure what it told him. All he knew was that Dan Foley had changed.

"I guess there is more to living than that," Johnny said after a long pause. "I thought for a little while I had found out what it was, but all I done was to make a fool out of myself."

"You done that, all right," Foley admitted. "The more I have to do with women, the less I know about 'em, but it looks to me like you can divide 'em into two classes, the ones like Myrtle who will do anything to get a man and the ones like Linda who use you any way they can and to hell with you."

Johnny didn't say anything. He couldn't. Just the mention of Linda's name drove a knife of agony through his middle. He didn't want to think of her or to think of any woman for that matter. He dropped a hand to the saddle horn and gripped it. A woman had used him and made a fool of him, so from now on he would use women in any way he could and to hell with the way they felt.

"We're wasting time talking about me," Foley said. "You're the one in trouble. I tell you what you do. If you ride straight west, you'll hit the South Platte and chances are you'll find a good place to camp. You'll have water and wood and grass for your horse. Why don't you hole up there till dark and catch up on your sleep? Tonight you can cross the river and keep going till you come to the mountains. You'll have to decide something then."

"Why should I travel at night?" Johnny asked. "I haven't committed any crime."

Foley stared at him a moment as if he thought he was a fool. He said, "Son, you've been in the same country with old Bull Tatum as long as I have. You oughta know how he navigates. He'll put men on your tail till one of 'em plugs you, or you get clean out of the country and shake 'em off."

"Well, you said while ago that if anybody was trailing us, they'd have showed up by now."

"All I meant was that if old Bull was home when Benny Quinn got there with the news of what happened, he'd have his crew saddle up and the whole kit and caboodle of 'em would be out fine-combing the country for you. Chances are he was over on the Frenchman like Al Frolich said, but he'll hear sooner or later. When he does, he'll hire a gunslick to hunt for you and keep on hunting till he finds you."

Johnny thought about it. He'd heard plenty about old Bull and he had seen him in town a few times, but he didn't actually know much about the man. Old Bull Tatum seemed more of a legend than a reality.

Foley knew him because his father was the second biggest cowman in the country and so was accepted by the Tatums and had often visited with them. Now that he thought about it, Johnny remembered that Foley had ridden for Rainbow a couple of times during roundup.

"You know what he'll do more'n I do," Johnny said, "but it seems to me that it's pretty hard for a man to hide his trail if somebody wants to pay enough to find him."

"Sure it's hard," Foley said, "but it can be done. That's why I said you'd have to decide something. You can go on across the mountains and get work in one of the mining camps, but if you're like me, you'd go loco staying down inside a tunnel all day and never seeing the sun. Another thing you might do is to go to Denver and get a city job, but you'd hate that as much as working in a mine. At least I would, with all the banging around there is in a big town and the crowds of people and such. You couldn't get a good deep breath."

"All right, so I'd best get me a job nursing cows like I've always done," Johnny said. "And where would I go so old Bull wouldn't find me?"

"Hell, man," Foley said, "the country is full of out-of-the-way places where you would never be found. Change your name. Just tell some rancher you're an experienced cowhand. You don't have to give him no pedigree."

"I ain't changing my name," Johnny said stubbornly. "If old Bull wants to find me, I'd better fix it so he can."

"If you want to die young, I guess that's a good way to do it," Foley said. "Was I you, I'd ride up the Poudre and go over Cameron Pass into North Park. Some big outfits up there. You won't have no trouble getting a job."

"Maybe I'll do that," Johnny said wearily.

Foley pulled up. "Time I was getting along."

Johnny stopped and held out his hand. "Go out and see Pa once in a while," he said. "He's the only one beside you I'm sorry about leaving. I should have gone home before I pulled out."

Foley shook his hand. "No, you done right. It's my guess some of the Rainbow boys have been out there before now. If you'd gone home, or if your pa knew anything about what happened and where you are, he'd be in a hell of a fix."

"Maybe so," Johnny said.

"You'd best cross the river and swing north of Greeley and Fort Collins," Foley said, "then hit the Poudre and keep going. You'll come to North Park."

"Why should I swing north of Greeley and Fort Collins?" Johnny asked.

"It's open country. Not many ranches. I'd say the chances were you'll get clean over Cameron Pass before anybody gets close enough to recognize you." He raised a hand in farewell as he turned his horse.

"Let me know when you get there. I won't even tell your pa where you are. I'll just say you're safe and well." He rode away, calling back, "Good luck, son."

Johnny went on, looking back only once to see Foley who had become a distant dot on the prairie. Then the loneliness settled down upon him, and it startled him to think how quickly and violently his life had been changed by what had happened within the last few hours.

The past months had been slow and draggy, with hard work through the week and a few hours in Star City on a Saturday afternoon. Maybe on Sundays some of the neighbors would drop in just to talk, all of them as frustrated as he was, imprisoned by the low sand hills, until sometimes he had thought he'd clench his fists and scream at the sky, or that he'd have to get out of the country just as he was doing.

Now it was different. He wished he could go back to those dull days when nothing much happened, back to the peaceful years of living with his father who was probably the only man in the sand hills who had made up his mind that this was the way of life he wanted and would continue to live to the day he died.

Johnny remembered asking Sherm Balder to tell his father that he would send for him as soon as he was settled. Now, with his mind perfectly clear, he knew it had been a foolish thing to say. His father would never leave the sand hills.

He reached the South Platte sometime in the afternoon. He found a cool camping place in a cottonwood grove, watered his horse and staked him out in the grass, then built a fire and cooked a meal. No one was around, he saw no cattle or horses, and as far as he could see there wasn't even a homesteader shanty in sight.

He thought of North Park where Foley suggested that he go. He'd heard of it, a high, wild valley between two chains of the Rockies, a perfect cattle country according to some of the stories he had been told. Whether the stories were exaggerated or not, he wanted to see it. If he liked it, he would stay if he found a job. If he didn't, he'd keep riding. It was a big world and he'd wanted to see what lay beyond the sand hills for a long time. Now he had his chance.

Not once did he think of Linda. He had built a wall around her and had dropped her into a deep recess in the back of his mind. He would never see her again. She meant nothing to him. Now that he thought about it, he didn't much care whether the Rainbow men found him or not.

Then he thought of something else. He had never been one to duck and run. It had been Foley's idea to take out across the empty country north of the South Platte, not his. He might just as well get back onto the road and ride through the towns and stay in hotels and put his buckskin up in livery stables.

He smoked a cigarette, the fire going out. The day

was a hot one with very little wind. He considered undressing and taking a swim, but suddenly the long ride and the night without sleep caught up with him. He'd sleep a couple of hours, he decided, then throw the saddle on the buckskin and ride upstream. The town of Fort Morgan was not far from here.

He picked up his saddle and, carrying it deeper into the grove, put it down beside a drift log. He lay down, his head on the saddle, and fell asleep at once. It seemed only a minute later when he heard his horse whinny. He woke to find that the sun was almost down. He heard the horse again, then the rustling of grass as someone moved cautiously toward him. So some of the Rainbow crew had caught up with him, he thought, and reached for his revolver.

– 8 –

For what seemed an eternity Johnny lay motionless, forcing himself to breathe lightly, his pistol gripped in his right hand. The footsteps came closer and then stopped. He pictured one of the Rainbow riders standing there with his revolver in his hand waiting for his man to show himself.

Then the thought struck Johnny that maybe the Rainbow man didn't know where he was. He had seen the buckskin, so had guessed that Johnny was around here somewhere, but there were a dozen drift logs along the bank, any of them big enough to hide a man. Or, for all the Rainbow rider knew, he might have been swimming and now was hiding behind the bank.

If Johnny showed himself, he would draw a bullet, but if he was guessing right, the Rainbow cowhand, standing out there in the open by himself, was in as much of a quandary as he was, perhaps even a worse one. The chances were he had seen the buckskin, had recognized it as Johnny's horse, and had ridden up, dismounted, and started looking before he had real-ized there was this tangle of driftwood and brush and a five- or six-foot bank at the edge of the river. Now he was caught in the open without the slightest idea where Johnny was, not knowing whether he had been seen or not, with his skin crawling in anticipation of a bullet anytime.

The Rainbow man would not stand out there much longer regardless of the way he took out of his dilemma. Johnny decided he had better break the impasse while he could and possibly gain an advantage that he would not have if the man moved around the drift log and discovered him.

Tensing his muscles, he rolled to one side and then on over on his stomach and propelled himself upright. He found himself facing a cowboy who was standing not more than twenty feet from him, a revolver in his hand. Surprised, the Rainbow rider fired, a snap shot that missed by three feet, then he panicked and dived headlong toward the drift log. He rolled toward it, keeping the log between him and Johnny who fired once and missed, the bullet kicking up dust inches behind the man just before he disappeared from sight.

Whirling, Johnny sprinted toward a cottonwood that stood between him and the bank. It was not until he reached it and stood with the big trunk between him and the Rainbow man that he realized the fellow was Jess Crowder, the Rainbow foreman. Johnny remembered Curly Mike Malone saying last night in Sherm Balder's office that it didn't make any difference whether old Bull was home or not, that Jess Crowder would be there and Crowder would do what old Bull would have done if he'd been home. That was exactly what had happened.

Johnny stepped to one side of the tree, his gaze sweeping the drift log. He had reversed the situation, and so had gained one big advantage; he knew where Crowder was and he could hold him there. He thought briefly of telling the Rainbow foreman to throw his gun over the drift log and stand with his hands up, then realized at once it would be a waste of breath. Jess Crowder was a younger edition of old Bull, far more like him than his own son Tom had been. Crowder had come here to kill Johnny Deere and he would do it or be killed. He was that kind of man.

In a few minutes the light would be too thin for accurate shooting. Johnny didn't want to play a game of powder-smoke hide-and-seek with Crowder in the darkness. Then another thought occurred to him, that there might be other Rainbow men strung out along the river hunting for him. If that were true, the sound of shots would draw them. He'd better get this over with, he decided, and ran away from the river toward the next cottonwood. There he paused and caught his breath.

The old familiar recklessness was crowding him again. He called, "This was your idea, Jess. Want to give up now and ride out of here in one piece?"

He angled toward the next tree, still moving away from the river so that he would eventually swing far enough around the drift log to see along the south side where Crowder was hiding. He was halfway between the trees when Crowder raised himself high enough to squeeze off a shot at Johnny, then dropped back at once. He saw the heavy blossom of smoke drift across the cottonwood and fired an answering shot that splintered the bark on top of the log. Then he reached the tree he had been running toward and paused behind it long enough to thumb two loads into the cylinder to replace the spent shells.

He was almost in line with the drift log, but he still couldn't see Crowder. The next tree was too far away. If he tried to reach it, he'd have a long run in the open and that was exactly what he didn't want to do. He was surprised that Crowder had let himself be caught without protection as he had.

Probably Crowder hadn't reasoned it out. He had seen the buckskin, Johnny guessed, and a driving urge to avenge Tom Tatum's death had caused him to wade in before he had taken time to size up the situation. Now he was pinned down along the side of the drift log just as Johnny had been a few minutes before.

Standing beside the tree, Johnny said, "How do you like it down there, Jess, with your nose in the dirt? Maybe you belong to the gopher family and purty soon you'll be digging your way under the log."

Suddenly and for no rational reason Johnny laughed. Neither Jess Crowder nor old Bull Tatum had ever been able to take any kind of hoorawing. Sooner or later he'd goad Crowder into showing himself. He picked up a rock and tossed it over the drift log, not sure whether he hit Crowder or not.

"You're a dead man, Jess," Johnny prodded. "You got yourself boxed, didn't you? I guess you ain't much smarter'n Tom was. He came after me with a knife and then killed himself with it. You sneak in here with a gun in your hand, and now you're going to get your hide ventilated instead of mine."

He paused, then picked up another rock and tossed it toward the drift log. It hit the far edge and skittered off. He said, "How do you like it, Jess, having rocks thrown at you? Ain't that a hell of a note for a tough hand like you who's always bossed folks around? Sooner or later I'll get lucky and hit you on that punkin head of yours and you'll be out cold." He paused again, and said slowly, "You're a coward, Jess, lying there hugging that log. I guess you've got the biggest yellow belly I ever seen on a man."

Crowder yelled an obscenity and jumped up, his gun roaring. He shot quickly, aiming at nothing except the sound of Johnny's voice. He missed, but Johnny didn't. His first shot caught Crowder in the left arm and spun him halfway around, the second drove through the foreman's belly and knocked him down.

Johnny ran toward him, keeping him covered. Crowder heaved up on his hands and knees, right hand groping for the gun he had dropped, then fell flat. Johnny reached him and turned him over. Crowder stared at him, the knowledge of death in his eyes, and still he had the strength to curse Johnny.

"Old Bull will keep somebody on your trail till he gets you," Crowder whispered. "You might just as well shoot yourself now. You'll never . . . make . . . it."

A moment later he was dead. Johnny holstered his gun and looked around. If other Rainbow men were hunting for him along the river, they apparently had been too far away to hear the shots. Now, staring at the dead man in the rapidly fading light, it struck Johnny that if the body were found he could be accused of murder. There were no witnesses. With old Bull Tatum having the power he did, Johnny's word spoken in his own defense would not amount to much.

He found a board with a sharp end that had drifted down the river. Using it as a shovel, he dug a shallow grave in the sand along the side of the drift log and dragged Crowder's body to the grave and rolled it into it. He filled the grave and, employing the board as a lever, he eased the log far enough toward the river to cover the grave. Taking a tree branch, he erased the footprints around the log and wiped out the trail the body had made when he'd dragged it through the sand.

He removed the bridle from Crowder's horse and gave him a slap on the rump with it. The animal would get back to Rainbow eventually, and by that time Johnny Deere would be a long way from here. Mounting his buckskin, he crossed the river.

The darkness was complete by now. He located the North Star and from it charted his course directly westward across the empty land. He remembered what Crowder had said just before he died, that old Bull Tatum would keep somebody on his trail till he was dead, that he'd never make it. Now he wondered if he would.

Two violent deaths had put him on the run and tempered the natural recklessness that was in him. The fact that one had been an accident and the other had resulted from his attempt to defend himself did not make the least bit of difference. What had happened to him, he thought bitterly, was the worst kind of miscarriage of justice.

They buried Tom Tatum Tuesday afternoon. The day was a hot one with no breeze whatever, but everybody in town and from the hard land to the north and up and down Pole Creek and out of the sand hills except Frank Deere was there. Even Benny Quinn and his wife and two babies were in the crowd, the babies whimpering because they had broken out in a heat rash.

Quinn had made five dollars by riding out to Rainbow Saturday night. Now he was afraid to not come to the burying. Most of the others were there for the same reason. But not Dan Foley. He was there because he was adding to an investment he had started to make several weeks ago.

Foley stood beside Linda Hollison, looking at her hungrily from time to time and still trying to keep the proper funereal expression upon his face. Linda held a handkerchief to her red-rimmed eyes, and now and then started to tremble uncontrollably. Then Foley would put out a hand to steady her and she would look at him gratefully and he would drop his hand. When this happened, Mrs. Hollison, standing on the other side of Linda, would turn her head and glare at him. He pondered this, a feeling growing in him that she was the only one in the crowd who saw through him and therefore was dangerous to his future.

He shrugged and turned his attention to old Bull Tatum who was standing beside the coffin. Mrs. Hollison was a woman and therefore could be taken care of any time it was necessary. Right now old Bull was the immediate problem and Foley hadn't made up his mind what was the best approach to make.

The choir from the Methodist church had sung "Nearer my God to Thee," and "In the Sweet By and By." Then the preacher stepped up to the open grave and began to pray in his usual long-winded style. This was a captive audience and by far the biggest crowd he had ever had, so, being a practical man, he made the most of it.

Foley kept his gaze on old Bull Tatum. He stood a full head shorter than Foley, and was built in a sort of triangle with small feet and skinny legs and a narrow waist, but with tremendous shoulders and hands and arms. His round bald head, glistening under the hot sun, was fastened to his shoulders without the visible support of a neck. He claimed he could knock a steer down with a single blow of his huge fist, and Foley was not inclined to challenge the statement.

Now it was plain that old Bull was becoming impatient. Finally he moved to the preacher and jerked on his coattail. Foley couldn't hear what he said, but it might have been "Turn it off." Foley wouldn't have been surprised if those were Tatum's words because the preaching was moving toward dangerous ground, imploring the Lord to have mercy on Tom Tatum's soul. Tom had never joined the church and been baptized, so the preacher was implying that Tom might be in an even hotter climate than the one here on Pole Creek.

The preacher said, "Amen" in a startled voice and stepped back, his face red. Old Bull motioned for the coffin to be lowered into the grave, and then, as the men began filling it and the first clod struck the coffin, he clapped his Stetson on his head and, turning, strode directly to Linda. Watching him, Foley was scared. Old Bull's face had become as dark and menacing as one of the funnel-shaped clouds that occasionally rushed through the Pole Creek country.

Old Bull stopped in front of the startled girl. He said in a great voice that everyone in the crowd heard, "You bitch! You Goddamned slut! If it wasn't for you Tom would be alive today." He raised a hand and struck her hard on the side of the face. The blow sounded like a dry twig breaking and sent Linda sprawling headlong onto the grass.

Old Bull took a deliberate step forward and brought his right boot back, evidently intending to kick her in the ribs. Quickly Foley moved between old Bull and Linda just as Mrs. Hollison screamed. Foley said in a low voice that no one heard except old Bull, "Did Jess Crowder's horse come back?"

Tatum blinked and lowered his right foot to the ground. He was startled and perhaps surprised that Foley had the temerity to step between him and Linda, but he was even more startled to learn that Dan Foley or anyone besides his crew suspected that Jess Crowder might not be alive.

"Yeah, the horse was back when I got home," Tatum said. "Why?"

Sherm Balder and Mrs. Hollison were helping Linda to her feet and half carrying her to the buggy that Mrs. Hollison had rented from Al Frolich. If old Bull noticed, he paid no attention. Foley said in a low tone, "Then Johnny Deere killed Jess. In a few days I'll ride out to Rainbow and see you."

"Don't bother," Tatum said. "If you've got anything to say, say it now."

"No," Foley said. "I have some information you want, and I'm the only one who has it. I'll give it to you in my own way and my own time."

He deliberately turned his back and walked to his horse. Mrs. Hollison was in the buggy beside Linda who was holding a hand to the side of her face. Doc Allen hurried to the buggy. He said, "I'll have a look at her as soon as you get her home."

Mrs. Hollison nodded, her gaze on old Bull who was stomping across the grass to his horse, his cowhands trailing behind him. She said to Sherm Balder, "Can't you arrest him? Or is he as big as God and above the law?"

"It's not that he's above the law," Sherm said wearily. "It wouldn't do any good if I tried to arrest him. He wouldn't be convicted. You know it as well as I do, Mary."

She didn't say anything more, but spoke to the horse and turned the buggy toward the road, Foley riding beside her and Linda who still sat motionless beside her mother, her handkerchief pressed to the side of her face where old Bull had struck her. They were not halfway to town when the Rainbow crew swept by on the run, Tatum in the lead, gray dust boiling up behind them in a great cloud.

Mrs. Hollison stopped until the dust settled, Foley pulling in close beside the buggy. The Rainbow outfit thundered across Pole Creek bridge and went on through town without slackening speed, and presently dust rose beyond Star City as the Rainbow riders started up the long slant beyond the town.

Mrs. Hollison went on, not saying a word until they reached her house. Foley dismounted and walked around the buggy to Linda's side. He said, "I'll take her into the house and then I'll drive the rig to the livery stable." Mrs. Hollison opened her mouth to say something, then closed it without saying anything, her gaze following Foley as he went into the house, holding Linda in his arms as tenderly as if she were a baby.

When he returned, she stepped out of the buggy

and handed the lines to him. She said, "I don't understand you, Dan. I just don't understand you at all."

He swung into the seat, smiling at her. "I'll be back. I want to see Linda and I want to talk to you."

When he returned, Mrs. Hollison met him at the door. "Come in, Dan," she said. "I'm sorry, but you can't see Linda. Doc Allen's with her. She's in bad shape, he says, and she'll have to be kept quiet for a long time. That . . . that monster hit her awfully hard and I thought he might have broken some bones in her face, but Doc doesn't think so. It's a shock, though, coming after seeing Tom killed the way he was. I didn't want her to go to the funeral, but she wouldn't listen."

He followed her into the front room and sat down on the black leather couch, his hat balanced on his knee. He stared at Mrs. Hollison for a long moment, debating about whether it was the right time and place to be honest with her. He was seldom honest with anyone, so it was a difficult decision for him to make.

"I have a feeling lately that you don't like me, Mrs. Hollison," he said slowly. "I risked my life today when I stepped between Linda and old Bull. For that reason if for no other I think I have a right to know what I've done to turn you against me."

"Yes, you have the right," she said. "I intended to thank you. You not only risked your life, but you may have saved Linda's. To think that he would do what he did and know he was perfectly safe and that the sheriff would not touch him is beyond belief." She swallowed, and then went on, "I don't know why you did it. I wonder if you ever let anyone know how you really feel about things or people."

She sat very straight with her hands folded on her lap. Now she raised a hand and wiped the sweat from her face with her handkerchief, then folded her hands again, her gaze never leaving Foley's face. Overhead a board creaked as Doc Allen walked around Linda's room, then there was silence except for the steady buzzing of a fly against a window.

"I don't think that's it," he said. "A lot of people don't let other folks know how they feel, but that doesn't make you dislike them. I'll admit that you're right about me not letting people know how I feel. You see, this is very important because I love Linda and I want to be sure it's all right with you for me to call on her as soon as she's able to see me."

She was still looking directly at him. "You've changed, Dan. I've noticed it in just the last few weeks. You were never serious about anything. I think you really are now."

"I haven't changed," he said earnestly. "I want you to know that I'm telling you exactly how I feel and it ain't easy." He stared at his hat, pausing as he thought about what he should say, then he looked up. "It's this way, Mrs. Hollison. Nobody ever took me seriously about anything. I'm ten years younger than my closest brother. My dad and brothers never let me do any-thing. They figured I couldn't, I guess. They always done my work for me and laughed at anything I tried to do, so I got to laughing back. I'd tell jokes and play crazy tricks, and I . . . I guess folks got to thinking of me as a sort of clown."

He lowered his head again and stared at his hat, thinking he had not intended to be as honest as he had, but it was said, and perhaps it was just as well. Then he added, "If you've seen any change in me, it's because I got tired of being looked at as a clown. When it came time to get Johnny out of town, the men listened to me. That's the way it's going to be. Give me enough time and I'll be the most important man on Pole Creek. I want Linda for my wife." He paused and swallowed, and then leaned forward. "Mrs. Hollison, if she'll have me, I'll make her a better husband than Tom Tatum ever would."

"Yes Dan, I believe you will. You asked why I didn't like you. All right, I'll tell you. I felt you were really to blame for what happened to Tom Tatum, not Linda or Johnny. She's not one to tell me everything that happens to her, but she said enough for me to know that you've been seeing her and telling her she had to show Tom who was boss before it was too late. It was your idea for her to hoodwink Johnny into taking her to the dance. If you thought it was such a fine idea, why didn't you take her?"

"For the same reason I just gave you," he said. "Would Tom Tatum or anybody else take the clown of Pole Creek seriously?" He shook his head. "You know they wouldn't. But Johnny . . ." He paused, hoping she would not sense the hatred he had for Johnny Deere. That was the last thing he wanted anyone to know. "Well, it was different with Johnny. The proddy way Tom came to the dance proves it. I didn't think it would work the way it did."

"But you knew Linda didn't love Johnny and you hoped your scheme would break her and Tom up, and then you'd have a chance with her."

It didn't sound right the way she said it, but it was true, and he decided that it was smart to keep on being honest with her. He nodded. "That's right. Tom wouldn't have been good for her. I think I will."

She rose. "I'd better go up and see how Linda's feeling."

"Then it's all right with you if I come to see Linda?"

She walked to the foot of the stairs and put a hand on the banister. She turned to look at him, then she said slowly, "Yes, you may come to see her."

He watched her climb the stairs, then walked out of the house into the afternoon heat. He was smiling as he stepped into the saddle. It had gone as well as he could expect. For once it had paid to be honest. He wondered if it would work with old Bull Tatum, too.

Johnny Deere rode west by night and slept by day, usually in a ravine where he had staked out his horse. This way he felt reasonably sure that neither he nor the animal would be visible to anyone going by. Occasionally he saw a light in a ranch house which beckoned to him and he had to fight the impulse to ride to it, to pose as a grub line rider and get a free meal or two and go on in the morning.

He always successfully defeated the impulse and rode on, but it was enough to make him think as he had never thought before. He had been lonely in the sand hills, and discontented with his life, discontented enough to make him ride into town Saturday filled with a crazy recklessness that alarmed his father and had made him risk life on a number of occasions.

What he had realized, and he was ashamed now, was the simple fact that his father loved him and had taken care of him in more ways than he had dreamed. Frank Deere was old and tired and a self-admitted failure, a man who had even lost his dreams and wanted nothing more than to live in peace in the sand hills until he died. *But he had always been there.* He had been someone to talk to, to work with, to fix their simple meals and do an occasional washing. Above everything else was the vital fact that his father cared about what happened to him. Now there was no one.

Guilt nagged at him for not seeing his father before he left the country. The only thought that gave him any relief was Sherm Balder's promise that he would ride out and see Frank Deere and tell him that Johnny would send for him when he was located. Not that his father would come, but it would let him know that Johnny had not just ridden off and left him.

So he rode, day after day, circling far north of the towns of Greeley and Fort Collins. He stopped once at a country store and bought supplies, and went on, thinking that if this gave old Bull Tatum a clue to his whereabouts, he was welcome to it. One thing was certain. Johnny Deere was not going to starve to death because he was afraid of old Bull Tatum's revenge.

He struck the Cache la Poudre above Fort Collins and turned west along it and rode into the mountains. He had an uneasy feeling when the walls of the canyon closed in upon him; he felt penned up, the way a wild animal must feel when he is placed in a cage.

Twice he put his buckskin up the steep slope that was the north wall of the canyon, wanting to see what was on the other side, and both times he returned to the bottom, disappointed. He had seen nothing except row on row of ridges, their rocky crests combing the sky.

To a man who had spent nearly all of his life on Pole Creek or in the low sand hills, it was unbelievable that there were so many mountains in the world.

They terrified him, for he was trapped with only two ways of escape: back down the river toward Fort Collins or westward toward North Park which was obviously the intelligent thing to do. He wanted to see the park; it was not a canyon like this and he would be able to breathe again.

He passed a fruit peddler who was headed for North Park with a load of apples, peaches, and melons. Later he met stockmen who were riding downstream and nodded to them, for now he rode by day and slept at night, refusing to take the precautions he had taken on his way to the mountains. Some of the ranchers, he judged, had come from North Park and were on their way to Fort Collins to transact business, but he did not take time to stop them and ask questions.

If old Bull Tatum had guessed he had come this way and had sent someone to inquire about him in Fort Collins, Tatum's man might pick up his trail if he happened to question the same rancher Johnny had talked to. This way he was only one of a number of travelers on the road and it seemed unlikely that anyone would remember him.

He started over Cameron Pass, the air becoming steadily colder as he climbed. He topped the summit and started down the western slope, the timber closing in around him. The road which was little more than a trail twisted and dropped ahead of him. Twice he came upon small bands of deer that bounded away and disappeared. Once he startled a small bear that seemed to tumble off the road and went smashing bull-like through the brush.

Johnny smiled and kept dropping with the trail. For some strange reason he liked it here, feeling none of the terror of being imprisoned that had burdened him on the other side whenever he had looked up at the high, steep slopes that walled in the canyon. He sensed the wildness here, a freedom he had never felt before, and he was reminded of a book he had read about the Swiss, mountain dwellers who refused to be conquered because they loved freedom so much they placed it above everything else.

Perhaps he imagined it, but it seemed to him that there was a mountain smell around him which was carried by the thin, cold air. He shivered and put his buckskin to a faster pace and presently reached a lower country, the timber still crowding him. He made camp at sundown on the Middle Fork of the Michigan, and drank the cold, pure water, wishing he had a pole and line. He had never fished for trout, but it was something he would do if he stayed in this country.

He heard many sounds that night, sleeping an hour and waking, and sleeping again. The night-chilled air was as cold as many winter nights in the sand hills. He kept the fire up, made uneasy by the murmurings in the brush around him. This was primitive country, untamed and uninhabited. If there were small bears in the region, he thought, there would be big bears, too, and hungry ones perhaps. Mountain lions more than likely, and wolves.

He was relieved when dawn began to brighten the sky above the peaks to the east, and he rose and built up the fire. He cooked breakfast, then rode west again. The day turned warm, but not hot, the air retaining a winy, bracing quality he had never felt before. Later he passed bunches of steers in green, lush meadows. Shorthorns mixed with native Texas cows, he guessed, and wondered why white-faces had not been introduced.

Presently he was out of the timber except for a few scattered pines and could look back at the tall peaks of the Medicine Bow range. That was when he heard the shooting.

He reined his buckskin to a stop, his head cocked as the sharp crack of rifles came to him. He wasn't sure of the direction for a moment, then decided the shooting came from somewhere to the north and farther east. As he sat in his saddle, a meadow lark's sweet song came to him from somewhere out in the grass. Overhead a hawk swooped and lifted again, carried by a vagrant wind current.

Johnny slapped at a mosquito that buzzed in his ear as he turned his horse north. Whatever was going on was not his fight and he would have no part of it. He'd just take a look to see what was going on and then he'd be riding. He'd been in enough trouble lately without buying into more before he even found a ranch where he could ask for a job.

He was in the timber again when he pulled up a few minutes later, a small bowl opening before him. The rifle shots were very close now. Leaving the buckskin ground-hitched, he pulled his Winchester from the boot and wormed his way to the rim. Most of the firing, he saw, was coming from the opposite side.

He peered over the edge and swore softly. An old man with a Santa Claus beard and mustache lay flat on his back behind a boulder. He had been hit hard, Johnny judged. He might even be dead. At least he wasn't moving, so it was unlikely that he had been doing any of the shooting. Not since he'd been hit anyhow. But someone had, or the men across from Johnny wouldn't remain holed up in a tangle of dead-falls as they were. He couldn't see them but from the amount of firing, he judged there were three of them.

For several minutes Johnny studied the boulders around where the old man lay before he saw who was shooting. He wouldn't have seen them if one of the men across the bowl hadn't showed himself. A rifle cracked immediately from the boulders. The man yelled and ducked out of sight.

Johnny saw her then, a slip of a girl lying between two of the boulders, her rifle barrel thrust through the narrow crack between them. He hadn't seen her before because she hadn't moved. She wore a gray-green riding skirt and jacket that was very close to the color of the grass and sagebrush around her.

Johnny sighed and pulled back, then began working his way around the rim. He was a sucker for trouble, he told himself sourly, but a man didn't have any choice in a situation like this.

— 1 1 —

Johnny worked his way back and forth through the deadfalls and brush along the rim. With the odds against him as they were, he knew that his one chance of winning was to surprise the three men. He had to cross a few open places where there was no cover. He was afraid he would be seen, but apparently he wasn't. At least he didn't draw their fire.

Only one thing saved him, he thought, the fact that the attention of the three men was fixed so closely on the girl in the bottom of the bowl that they were not looking around. Obviously they did not think anyone else was in the country and so did not expect interference.

Once during a lull in the firing one of the men yelled, "All we want is the money, Sally. You know damn well we don't want to hurt you. We didn't aim to hit Tuck."

Her answer was another shot which drove the

speaker flat on his face behind the deadfall. Johnny couldn't hear what the man next to him said, but it was something about it wasn't any use, then "get on the other side" and finally "smoke her out."

Johnny had wondered about that from the moment he'd first seen what was happening. The girl had almost perfect protection from the men's rifle fire as long as they remained on the east side of the bowl, but if one of them moved to the opposite rim, they'd get at her from both sides and she'd be dead. The shooting had been going on for half an hour or so. To Johnny it seemed stupid not to wind the affair up but maybe these were stupid men.

He was close to them now, close enough to hear snatches of their talk as they argued, one of them saying that if they killed the girl, they'd have every man in North Park on their tail and they'd wind up swinging on the end of a rope, but robbing her wouldn't start any big trouble. One of the other two said they'd be out of the country long before anyone found the girl's body, that everybody thought she and her grandpa had started for Fort Collins and they wouldn't even start looking for her until next month. He'd put a slug in her without worrying about her being a girl. She'd been too smart for her pants for a long time and he was willing to give her what she had coming.

Johnny had not been able to stand up and take a look at the position of the two men, but from what he had seen and heard, he judged they were just beyond the next deadfall. Apparently a vicious twister had slashed through here not long before and had uprooted almost every spruce for nearly a quarter of a mile along the east rim.

From here on he faced a jungle that he couldn't possibly get through without showing himself. He felt that whatever he did he had to do now while the three men were still together. From the argument he guessed this situation wouldn't last much longer.

The girl was firing now and then, probably on general principles in the hope of keeping her enemies pinned down. Johnny waited until she shot again and one of the men fired back. He cocked his rifle, the sound covered by the firing. He rose and raced around the roots of the deadfall, calling, "Hook the moon, all of you."

One minute they were belly flat behind a log, their attention fixed on the girl and their own wrangling; the next they exploded into startled action. One of them leaped to his feet and was knocked down the next instant with a bullet in his head. The girl had been watching and had acted instinctively and accurately. A second man did not panic, but made a frantic effort to swing his rifle barrel around to shoot Johnny. He died beside the log where he lay, Johnny's slug smashing his heart.

The third man ran. He sailed over the nearest log in

a tremendous leap, fell on his face and was up again at once, crashing through the brush, ducking and dodging and twisting as he ran toward his horse that was tied with two others in the standing timber to the east. Johnny fired twice and missed, and shook his head as he watched the fear-crazed man fight his way headlong through the tangle of downed logs and limbs and roots.

I could have stopped him, Johnny thought. *I could have killed him. Why didn't I?*

He stood watching until the man reached his horse and fled through the trees. He knew the answer to his question. He hadn't tried to hit him. He couldn't bring himself to kill a man by shooting him in the back. As he turned to look at the two who had been shot, he knew this was a weakness which might sometime in the future get him killed.

The men sprawled behind the log were dead. The one the girl had shot was middle-aged with a white mustache, the other was bearded but much younger. They looked alike and Johnny judged that they were father and son. The one who had escaped was prob-ably a younger son. From the glimpse he'd had of the fellow, Johnny thought he was not over twenty.

Johnny moved toward the rim, knowing that if he showed himself the girl would shoot him. He thought about it a moment, then called, "The men up here won't hurt you any more. Two of them are dead and the third one got away." The girl remained silent. Presently he shouted, "You need any help?"

When she didn't answer, he thought to hell with it. She could stay down there until night if it made her feel any safer. He could understand why it would. He worked his way through the fallen trees to where the two horses were tied and pulled off the saddles and bridles and turned them loose. He returned to his buckskin, keeping well back of the rim.

He hesitated, not sure he was doing the right thing in leaving her. He bellied up to the rim and looked down. Neither she nor the old man had moved. He called, "Miss, I'm on the west side where I was when I first seen you. I'm leaving now unless you want some help."

She jerked her rifle out of the crack between the two boulders and dived behind a smaller one that hid her from Johnny's sight. Indignant, he shouted, "I ain't fixing to hurt you. You've got no call to be scared of me." She still said nothing and he realized that she might think she had exchanged one danger for another that could be greater.

"I turned their horses loose," he called. "In case you don't know who the men were who were trying to rob you, one of 'em's middle-aged with a white mustache and the other one's younger and has a beard. I figure he's a son. Looked like the one who got away was the youngest."

He drew back, not waiting for her to speak. Mounting, he rode west through the scattered timber and presently came out into the open country that ran before him mile after mile. The grass, he thought, was as good as he had heard. The winters would probably be ring-tailed wowsers, but the stockmen apparently knew how to bring their herds through the bad weather or they wouldn't survive.

An hour later he came to what he thought was only a ranch, but when he reined up and tied, he saw that the building on the east side of the road was a store and post office, the weathered sign in front informing him that this was Tucker.

The ranch house, barn, sheds, and corrals were across the road. A creek, spilling down from the Medicine Bows, slowed now that it had reached the floor of the park and meandered slowly toward the North Platte. Hay meadows lay on both sides of the stream, with a number of new stacks scattered for a mile or so along the creek.

He turned into the store, the name Tucker nagging him, then he remembered that one of the men on the west rim saying he hadn't wanted to shoot Tuck. It seemed quite likely that he might be the owner of the store and the ranch.

A tall man with inordinately long legs came out of the gloom in the back of the store. He squinted at Johnny, then he said, "What'll you have, stranger?"

"Information, I guess," Johnny said. "Who does this layout belong to?"

The slim man scratched the back of his skinny neck, his gray eyes on Johnny for a long moment before he said, "Who the hell wants to know?"

"I'm Johnny Deere." He held out his hand. "I've got a good reason for asking."

"I'm Highpockets Logan," the slim man said. "All right, I'll tell you and then you'd better give me that good reason you've got for asking on account of nosey gents ain't no more welcome in this country than the buffler gnats that eat you to pieces. The store belongs to old Tuck Tucker who came to this country before they laid the chunk. The spread across the road is the Double T and it's his'n, too."

"He's got a white beard and mustache?" Johnny asked. "And a girl who's wearing a greenish gray jacket and riding skirt and can shoot the eyes out of a chipmunk at fifty paces?"

"Right as rain," Logan said. "They started for Cameron Pass this morning. The gal, she's old Tuck's granddaughter. Sally Tucker, her name is. Right pert girl. The way she can handle a Winchester is a caution."

"Were they carrying considerable dinero?"

Logan eased along the counter toward a rifle that hung on the wall. "Talk quick and plain, mister, or by grab, I'll . . ."

"You won't do nothing," Johnny said. "Just answer my question."

"Yeah, they had some dinero," Logan admitted sullenly. "They was fixing to buy some supplies for the store so it could be freighted in afore snow fell and blocked the pass. Tuck was carrying it. Now will you tell me . . ."

"They was held up by three men and the old one got plugged," Johnny said, and told Logan what happened. He finished with, "I figured the girl needed help with the old man shot and being down in the bottom like they was, but she didn't trust me. I was afraid to go down to where she was. She wouldn't even answer when I hollered at her."

Logan's face turned red with anger. "I told Tuck to let me take the money. He's too old to be riding from here to Fort Collins and taking Sally with him. . . ." He stopped and leaned forward to peer suspiciously at Johnny, "If I thought you was the one that shot the old man and tried to plug Sally . . ."

Johnny wheeled toward the door. Logan called, "Wait." When Johnny turned back, he said, "I'm sorry. I guess you'd have kept going if you had anything to do with it. I'll harness up and go after 'em in the wagon. I know the bowl you're talking about. It's called Hogan's Hole. I'll haul Tuck in and I hope he's still alive. What did the hombres look like who done the shooting?"

Johnny described the dead men, and added, "I didn't get a good look at the one who got away, but he was a young, long-legged galoot. Maybe about twenty."

Logan swore angrily. "The Smelsers as sure as I'm a foot high." He swore again. "That was Wash who got away. Ike's the pappy and the other one's the oldest boy, Trig." He stopped to swear a third time. "The sons of bitches. They was our hay crew. They worked up till last night. They've got a cabin back in his hills. They took off after supper, saying they had to look for some horses that got away. They'd be back tomorrow, they said. Hell's bells, they never intended to do no such thing. They knowed Tuck and Sally was starting this morning and they knowed they'd have all that dinero on 'em."

He pulled the door shut and started across the road. Johnny asked, "Where's the county seat?"

Logan jerked a hand to the west. "Foller the road." He swung back. "Say, if you killed one o' the Smelsers, you'd best report it to the sheriff."

"I figured to," Johnny said and, mounting, rode west.

"Send Doc Rawls out," Logan yelled after him. "I'll have Tuck home afore dark."

"I'll send him," Johnny said, and rode on.

J ohnny reached Walden, the county seat, late in the afternoon. It was a small town, smaller even than Star City, spilling haphazardly along its Main Street. The buildings were frame except the bank which was brick. It lay on top of a small ridge, a ring of mountains surrounding it, but they were miles away.

He found Doc Rawls's office and dismounted in front of it and tied. He could learn to love this country, he thought, for here a man had room to move and breathe and live. As he turned into the medico's office, he told himself he would try every outfit in the park until he found a job, and then he realized with regret that he might not find anything permanent as late in the season as this.

Doc Rawls listened to what Johnny had to say and then grunted, "Jumpin' Judas, I've told that old fool Tuck a dozen times if I've told him once that he's not young any more and he's got to quit sashaying around over the country the way he does. He's as tough as a boot heel, but even a boot heel can get old."

"I guess any man's hide ain't young enough to stop a bullet," Johnny said.

"You're right about that, but it don't give him no excuse to ride around like he was twenty." The doctor glowered at Johnny, and then asked, "How'd you happen to buy into the ruckus?"

"I heard the shooting and thought I'd find out what it was all about," Johnny said. "I didn't intend to buy into any ruckus, but when I seen they had a girl pinned down, I figured I couldn't do nothing else but buy into it."

"Commendable, young man, commendable." Rawls took a hitch on his belt to bring his pants higher over his expansive belly, but they dropped back to their former position the instant he released them. "I'll try the question over again. I know everybody in North Park and I don't know you, so you're a stranger. What were you doing riding by Hogan's Hole?"

"I'm looking for a job," Johnny said shortly, and turned toward the door, nettled by the questioning.

"Hold on, boy, hold on," Rawls boomed, grinning a little. "I'm going out there right now to see if Tuck's still alive, and if he is, I can probably pull him through. Now I'll tell you something that'll save you a little time. You won't find no job in the park this time of year except back there on the Double T. High-pockets kind o' figures he's the ramrod and he makes it tough on any man who hires out to the Tuckers. I ain't sure why. Might be on account of he worries about Sally and he figures Tuck is too easy with her."

"All right, I'll go back and ask for a job," Johnny said. "I'll get along with Logan."

"Good." Rawls took another hitch on his belt. "I wish you would. You're a fighting man and that's what Tuck and Sally need. Highpockets ain't much when it comes to fight. Two men can run the outfit, but Highpockets chased the second rider off a month ago. They never should have hired the Smelsers for haying. Tuck and everybody else knows they're outlaws, so what they done ain't real surprising."

Rawls clapped on his hat, picked up his black bag, and left his office. Johnny followed him to the sidewalk and watched him move down the street to the livery stable in a kind of rolling gait. He probably did know everybody in the park, Johnny thought, and very likely watched over them the way a rooster watches over his flock. Johnny stood there until Rawls left the stable in his buggy and turned eastward toward the Double T, then he crossed the street to the post office, thinking that the doctor had tried to tell him something without putting it directly into words, but Johnny was not able to put his finger on it.

He wrote a note to Dan Foley, telling him he was in North Park and thought he could get a job. If he did, he would stay. He reminded Foley to tell his father he was all right, but for Foley not to say where he was. He didn't want his father tortured by old Bull Tatum or any of his men trying to make him tell where they'd find Johnny.

He sealed the envelope and stared at it a moment,

thinking of his father who, like Sherm Balder, had done so much for Star City and deserved peace of mind and enough money at his stage of life to make his last years easy. If Frank Deere had any peace of mind, it was because he had accepted defeat, and so did not strive for anything that was beyond his means. Johnny knew that his hasty departure was bound to hurt his father, but it would have hurt him more if he had stayed and old Bull Tatum had burned the town and killed him. He hoped his father understood that.

He mailed the letter, then asked when it would go out. "In the mornin' on the Laramie stage," the postmaster said. "Ain't no fancy stage. Just a plain old spring wagon, but it'll get there sooner or later." He peered over his steel-rimmed spectacles at Johnny. "Stranger in North Park, ain't you?"

"That's right," Johnny said, and walked out, thinking that the postmaster wanted to ask the same questions Doc Rawls had asked a few minutes before.

He found the sheriff in his office in the courthouse and told him what had happened, and then to stop the inevitable questions, he added, "I'm a stranger in North Park. I'm looking for a job, and I'm going back to the Double T and ask for one, and I aim to do my damnedest to get along with Highpockets Logan."

The sheriff threw back his head and laughed. He rose and put out his hand. "I'm Joe Veal. I ain't as nosey as Doc is, and I ain't as long on offering advice as he is. The truth is he's got a woman's tongue in a man's body and sometimes that leads to trouble, but he's got the best of intentions."

Veal was a small man about thirty, with hard, bunched muscles and the face of a Boston bulldog and a nature just as stubborn, Johnny guessed. He liked the man immediately, and was convinced that he would not back off from anything. He sensed none of the helplessness that was so much a part of Sherm Balder, and he could not keep from conjecturing what would happen if Joe Veal were sheriff in Star City.

"If it's all right with you," Johnny said, "I'll get something to eat."

"No, I want you to go with me to the Double T and we'd best get started," Veal said. "Sally will feed us if she's home, and if she ain't, we'll cook up something ourselves. To tell you the truth, I'm a little worried about that son of a bitch of a Wash Smelser getting away. I wish you'd shot him in the back or anywhere else. He was born to hang sooner or later, but he may do a lot of damage before we get an excuse to put a rope on his neck."

"This Logan . . ."

"Noise and bluster," Veal said sharply. "That's all. If he fought like he talks, he'd be hell on high red wheels, but he can't." He took a Winchester off the rack, checked it, and turned to face Johnny. "I'll try to run young Smelser down and I'd appreciate you going with me, at least to where you left the bodies of his pa and brother. I doubt that we catch him, though. He knows them mountains like his own backyard."

On the ride to the Double T, Johnny told Veal why he had left home. He thought there was a chance that Sherm Balder might be pushed into sending out wanted notices by old Bull Tatum, and it would be better if Veal heard the story from him first. Too, he appreciated the sheriff not asking questions the way Doc Rawls and the postmaster had.

Veal listened closely, and when Johnny had finished, he said: "I've heard about that situation over there. In fact, I went to Star City a couple of years ago to see a man Sherm Balder had in jail. I thought he was wanted in this county for horse stealing, but he wasn't the right man. I can savvy why Balder would be anxious to move you out of the country. Be easier to avoid trouble with you gone."

"If Sherm wants me, I suppose you'll have to send me back?"

Veal shrugged. "We'll cross that bridge when we come to it. You don't look like a liar and you don't talk like one. What's more, I don't think Balder will do that." He chewed on his lower lip a moment, then added: "It's my guess it's more likely some gunslick will show up looking for you. If he does, it becomes my problem and don't you forget it."

"If he gets to me first," Johnny said, "I don't figure

to stand still while he's shooting me."

"No," Veal said, grinning. "I guess that'd be too much to ask of any man."

They reached the Double T after dark, Highpockets Logan coming out of the house to meet them. "I'll take care of your horses," he said. "I reckon you won't be starting out to hunt for Wash Smelser tonight or to fetch the bodies in, neither, with it being as dark as the inside of a bull's gut like it is."

"No," Veal said shortly. "How's Tuck?"

"Alive," Logan said. "Had a slug in him that Doc just now dug out. I had a hell of a time getting him up out of Hogan's Hole. Had to leave the wagon on the rim. We finally made it, though. Doc figures he'll hang and rattle."

Johnny fell into step with Veal as the lawman strode to the house. He sensed the dislike that Veal had for Logan and wondered about it, but it was not a question he could ask at the time.

Veal opened the front door and called, "Sally."

She came out of the kitchen at once. "Come in, Joe." She looked past him at Johnny and asked, "Is this the man who saved my life?"

"That's him," Veal said. "Johnny Deere. Johnny, meet Sally Tucker, the best cook and the best rifle shot in North Park."

"You're overdoing it, Joe." She walked to Johnny and extended her hand. "Thank you. I apologize for not answering you when you hollered at me. I have no excuse for not answering except to say I was scared. I thought you must have heard about the money and I hadn't seen you, so I was afraid I was jumping from the frying pan into the fire."

She was a small blonde girl about twenty, Johnny judged, with a trim figure and the straightforward manner of a person who never ducks an issue. He instinctively liked her just as he had liked Joe Veal when he first met him, and the knowledge hit him with almost breathtaking impact that he wanted to work here and live in the park, that these were the kinds of people he wanted to be with.

"I understand," he said. "That's why I didn't push at you any more than I did."

She smiled as she turned back to the kitchen. "Had supper, Joe?"

"No," he said. "I told Johnny we'd wait for some of your good cooking."

"Not so good tonight," she said. "I didn't leave much in the house to eat. I thought we were on our way to Fort Collins."

"We'll take what you have." Veal nodded at Johnny. "He's looking for a job. How about it?"

She pinned her gaze directly on Johnny then, her head tipped back so she gave the impression of pointing with her chin. "If you're too proud to wrap your hands around the handle of a pitchfork, no. If you're willing to work, yes. I'll take Joe's word on you. I've never known him to be wrong about a man."

"Thanks," he said. "I'm not too proud to work."

"Good," she said in a businesslike way.

He followed her into the kitchen and, sitting down at the table, watched her work around the stove as she prepared their supper. He could not keep from thinking how completely different she was from Linda Hollison, or, for that matter, from every other girl he had ever known.

— 1 3 —

Dan Foley waited until he heard from Johnny and knew for sure he was in North Park and would probably stay. Then he saddled up and rode north to Rainbow. He had learned to wait. It had been the story of his life. He'd had to wait to grow up, wait to learn to ride and use a rope and a gun and to gain the other skills any cowhand must have. Most of all, he had waited to be accepted as a man by his family. Sometimes when he thought about it, the bitterness in him was so great that it was a poison making him physically sick.

He was big and he was strong, and he finally learned to do the things he had to do, learn them well enough to ride roundup for Rainbow two different years. His older brothers were married and had children. Both families lived with him and his father and mother in a rambling ranch house on Pole Creek six miles above Star City.

They got along with each other reasonably well, with Pa Foley ruling the family as a patriarch. None of them ever bothered to ask what Dan thought or felt about anything. Pa Foley gave him money whenever he asked for it. He worked when he wanted to and he came and went when he wanted to without any real responsibility.

The rest of the Foleys were tolerant of anything he did, so tolerant that he could not remember ever having had a whipping. His family said he had a great sense of humor. As far as he could tell, they seemed to think he was a little on the simple side with one talent and no more. He could make people laugh.

He honestly did not know why at the age of twenty-three he was still regarded as a boy. He did know that if he was ever to be accepted as a man, it had to be now. His family along with everybody else on Pole Creek would be surprised, but he had learned something the night Tom Tatum was killed, that when he set out to make something happen, he could get the job done, and when he spoke with a voice of authority, men listened.

On the afternoon Tom Tatum was buried, he had stood up to old Bull and saved Linda from a brutal kicking. That, he discovered, was the most amazing thing his folks had ever seen him do. Then, a short time later, he had been listened to by Mrs. Hollison.

Now, dismounting in front of the Rainbow ranch house, he knew exactly what he was going to do and he was a little giddy with a new sense of power. He tied, dropped a hand casually to the butt of his gun, and walked across the bare yard to the front door. He knocked, and when Slow Sam, the Negro cook and general handyman, came to the door, he said, "I want to see Mr. Tatum."

Slow Sam glanced toward the door of the room that was old Bull's office and shuffled his feet nervously. "I dunno 'bout that, Mistuh Foley. He ain't seein' nobody since young Tom died."

"He'll see me," Dan said, and pushed past Sam and strode toward old Bull's office.

Before he was halfway there, Slow Sam came unglued and, putting on a burst of speed which Dan didn't think he was capable of, ran past him to the door. "Mistuh Tatum, this . . ."

Old Bull half rose from his swivel chair as Foley pushed Sam aside and went into the room. "I wanted to see you, Mr. Tatum. I wasn't going back till I did."

Old Bull dropped back into his chair, his little, black eyes sparkling with anger. "By God, Foley, if you think you can bust into my house like you owned it, you're loco. Throw him out, Sam."

"Yes, suh," Sam said. "Right away, suh."

But he didn't move and Foley laughed. He said: "Before you have a heart attack and scare Sam to death by giving him a job he can't do, I'd best remind you what I said the afternoon Tom was buried. I have some information you want. I'm here to trade it to you."

Old Bull blinked and scratched behind an ear, then he picked up a short-stemmed pipe and filled it. "All right, Sam," he said. "I'll handle this."

"Yes, suh," Slow Sam said with relief, and disappeared into the back of the house.

"Let's have it," old Bull said brusquely. "I'm busy."

"Not too busy to talk to me," Foley said.

He dropped into a chair and rolled a cigarette as he glanced around the room. It was littered with pipes, tobacco cans, tally books, saddles, guns and various other items. This was old Bull's sanctum sanctorum, a room that probably had not been cleaned out since the house was built. Obviously Tatum was not a man to throw anything away.

Foley had never been here before. When he had ridden roundup, he had slept in the bunkhouse with the rest of the crew and eaten in the cook shack or was out on the range, and when he had visited here with his family as they did on special occasions such as Thanksgiving and Christmas, he stayed in the big front room or the dining room.

Tom Tatum and Jess Crowder had slept in the ranch

house. Crowder had taken his orders from old Bull and then had passed them on to the crew. Now Foley wondered who was foreman and how old Bull was getting along with his men. It was true that when Tom was killed, old Bull had been on the Frenchman with most of the crew, but that had been an unusual situation. Either Crowder had been given some job that had kept him here, or old Bull had wanted to look over personally the steers that he was buying.

Tatum remained at his desk, his face getting redder by the second. Finally he slammed a hand palm down against the desk top, a hard blow that rattled everything in the room. "Foley, I don't know who the hell you think you are. Just because you're Rip Foley's son you ain't got the right to shove your way into my house when I don't feel like talking to nobody."

Foley took the cigarette out of his mouth. "Mr. Tatum, do you want Johnny Deere dead?"

Old Bull wilted. In a matter of seconds he looked twenty years older than he had when Foley entered the room. He stared at his big hands that were spread on his desk, then he said slowly: "I want him dead so bad that I can't sleep at night. I can't even enjoy a meal no more. I'll pay you any amount you want if you'll tell me where that bastard is."

Foley rose and, walking to the desk, dropped his cigarette stub into the spittoon. He said, "Mr. Tatum, you've lost Tom and Jess Crowder. Now you need somebody, and I aim to be that somebody. I don't want to ramrod your outfit, but I want to be your partner in a general sort of way, a partner who does the things you need done when you don't want to do them yourself."

"I don't need nobody," old Bull bellowed. "I tell you, Foley, I don't know what you've been eating, but it ain't good for you."

"All right," Foley said, and turned to the door.

"Hold on," Tatum roared. "What kind of things do you think you can do for me? Why, hell, I can hire . . ."

"Sure, you can hire a lot of men," Foley said, "but you can't hire anybody like me. I've never amounted to much in this country, and I guess you know why, but from now on I'm going to cut quite a swath. I'll start by getting rid of Johnny Deere for you. I'll be the next sheriff. You need a man in that office, Mr. Tatum, not a gob of mush like Sherm Balder. We'll start by you having Sherm appoint me deputy. He don't have one, so it ought to be easy. Then you'll suggest that it's time he retired and you'll see that I'm appointed."

"You? Sheriff?" Tatum didn't seem to know whether to scowl or laugh, but he finally laughed, a short, guffawing sound. "I guess you're about the last man in the country I want to be sheriff."

"Suppose you let me start by serving as deputy before you make up your mind," Foley said. "There's some more things that I think you'd like. What do you want to happen to Frank Deere?"

"I want him dead, too," Tatum snapped. "Or out of the country anyhow. I don't ever want to hear the name Deere again."

"What about the girl, Linda?"

"I want her punished," Tatum said. "I don't care how."

"All right, I can take care of things like that for you," Foley said. "From what I hear you haven't done anything from the day Tom was killed except sit on your butt right here in this room. I guess you don't want to risk your reputation. Or maybe you're afraid. Maybe you don't know where to find a man who can be trusted." Foley tapped his chest. "I'm that man."

Tatum leaned back, his big hands clenching into fists and then opening and clenching again. Finally he said, "I thought you were Johnny Deere's friend?"

"He thinks so, too," Foley said, "but that don't prove nothing. I guess I hate him about as much as you do."

"Why?"

"Never mind why," Foley said impatiently. "Let's just say you 'n' me can use each other. I'll never sell you out and I'll never let you down."

Tatum rose and walked to a window, moving as slowly and ponderously as a Percheron stud. He asked, "How do we start?"

"I know where Johnny is," Foley said. "Give me

one thousand dollars and I'll use it to see he's rubbed out. I won't do it personally because I don't want to be gone from here that long, but I'll see that it's done. You'll speak to Sherm Balder about me being his deputy within the next day or so. Finally I'll be on your payroll for a hundred dollars a month, at least until I start drawing a salary as sheriff."

"All right," Tatum said, "but if you tell anyone about this arrangement, I'll deny it and I'll run you out of the country."

"You won't run me anywhere, Mr. Tatum," Foley said softly. "The day for folks thinking I don't count are gone. Now get me the dinero including my hundred dollars."

Old Bull seemed dazed as he walked to the safe in the corner of the room, opened it, counted out the money, and dropped it into the buckskin bag. When he handed it to Foley, he said, "I think you've gone whacky, but if you can do the things you say you can, it may work out for both of us."

"I'll do them," Foley said, and left the house.

On the way back to town, Foley thought about what his father had said many times, that when a man like old Bull Tatum once made his reputation as a brutal and ruthless man, he didn't have to go on proving it. Tom had been a weakling, and it was Foley's guess that he had been driven to attack Johnny at the dance because his father had needled him about that very thing until he had to prove both to himself and his father that he wasn't a weakling.

It seemed to Foley that Jess Crowder had been the key man, that old Bull's strength had laid in his foreman who had been with him from the time he had moved into the Pole Creek country. If that were true, and from the way he had reacted today, Foley was reasonably sure that it was, then old Bull was going to need a new man and Dan Foley would be that man.

As he rode through town he considered seeing Linda, but the last time he had talked to her mother, he was told she wasn't able to see anyone yet. She wasn't in sight when he rode past the house, so he went on to the courthouse, dismounted, and walked into Sherm Balder's office. It seemed to him that Sherm had been a little jumpy the last few days since Johnny had left.

"Howdy, Dan," Sherm said, when he saw who his visitor was.

The tone, Foley thought, was not friendly. He sat down, saying, "Howdy, Sherm," and wondered how everybody felt about turning against Johnny and practically running him out of town. Not just Sherm Balder, but Doc Allen and Curly Mike Malone and Dakota Sam Weeks and the rest. There might come a day, he thought, when they'd wish Johnny was back in town.

"Heard anything from Johnny?" Sherm asked.

"Not a word," Foley said blandly. "I figure he

won't live long. Old Bull will put a killer on his trail and keep him there until he catches up with him."

Sherm sighed. "I'm afraid you're more'n half right."

"Been out to see Frank?"

Sherm nodded. "I've been out there a couple of times. He's purty well cut up about Johnny leaving without even saying so long. He don't look well. I've got a feeling he won't live through the winter."

"No, probably not," Foley agreed. "You know, Sherm, you ain't looking real good lately, neither. You need a deputy. I'll serve without pay for a while because I aim to run for sheriff when your term's up and it might be a good idea for folks to start seeing me with a badge on my shirt."

Sherm froze, his gaze on Foley as if wondering whether he were serious. Finally he said, "I don't think you can do the job, Dan."

"I figure I can," Foley said. "I'm leaving for Denver in the morning. I'll pick up a badge when I get back."

He walked out, leaving Sherm staring at him as he left the office. He laughed as he stepped into the saddle and rode upstream toward the Foley ranch. He'd have his badge when he got back. A lot of folks would get a surprise, including his pa and a couple of know-it-all brothers. They just might find themselves in the calaboose one of these days.

J ohnny spent three days with Joe Veal combing the hills and mountains east of North Park for Wash Smelser. He wasn't sure whether the sheriff really thought he would find the outlaw, or whether he was going through the pretense of hunting for him while he was actually getting acquainted with Johnny.

In any case, he was sure that if Veal decided he was the wrong man to work for the Double T, he would say so flat out and Johnny would be smart to ride on. The more he saw of the short, stocky lawman, the more certain he was that Joe Veal would be the best of friends and the most ruthless of enemies.

The Smelser shack was in a narrow canyon several miles east of the Double T. Johnny and Veal found it empty. There was no sign that anyone had been there lately except that the shelves were stripped of food.

"They've been staying at the Double T while they were haying for Tuck," Veal said. "They don't run no cattle, and the horses are in that big pasture yonder with plenty of water, so they don't need looking after. Now it's my guess that Wash stopped for some grub and then sloped out of here. I don't have no idea where he'll go now."

"What did the Smelsers do to make a living?"

Johnny asked. "They couldn't make much out of a layout like this."

"No, they sure couldn't," Veal agreed, "Oh, they'd work for some of the park ranchers like they was haying for Tucker. They wasn't lazy. It's just that they didn't seem to have no ambition for themselves."

Veal cocked his head and studied the ridges on both sides of the canyon. "That bastard might be hiding up there. Maybe he's got us in his sights right now. If he was sure it was you, he'd pull the trigger. The Smelsers had a great notion about being loyal to each other. It's about the only good thing I can say 'bout 'em besides being willing to put out a day's work for whoever hired 'em." He paused, and asked, "Want to go back?"

"No," Johnny said, and wondered if that was part of Joe Veal's testing.

The sheriff grunted something and, stepping into the saddle, rode upstream. Presently he said, "We've all thought the Smelsers were bank robbers or horse thieves or something. They'd go away for two, three months sometimes, and nobody would ever find out where they'd been. Usually they'd come back with a bankroll big enough to choke a bull, but they never opened their mouths about where or how they'd got it. All I've been able to do is to keep an eye on 'em, but this is the first time we ever caught 'em at anything we could hold 'em for."

"Sally recognized 'em," Johnny said thoughtfully. "Seems funny they'd try to rob her. They knew she'd tell you, didn't they?"

"They never intended for her to talk to nobody," Veal said harshly. "You said you heard 'em arguing, with old Ike wanting to rub her out and Trig wanting to let her live. The thing is Trig tried his damnedest to go with her, but she wouldn't do it. Ike would have had his way when the time came. He always did."

Johnny had a strong suspicion that any man who went with Sally would come under the sharp observation of all the park people. Gradually as Veal talked Johnny's suspicions were verified. They camped the second night near the head of the North Fork of the Michigan.

After they had eaten supper, the sheriff said, "I reckon I've said enough for you to figure out that all of us think a hell of a lot of Sally and Tuck. You see, Tuck's one of those old boys who makes you think he's a saint who just stepped out of the Bible. He's helped most everybody in the park in one way or another. Loaned us money. Sold us hay if we got into a pinch. Used to preach at our funerals before we had a preacher in the park. Even doctored us until Doc Rawls moved in here from Laramie."

Veal tossed a chunk on the fire and stared at it a moment, then he said, "He had a son who was married. They lived with him and we all thought they got along fine. Then they had some kind of a row. None of us ever found out what it was about. The son and his wife pulled out and went to live in Fort Collins. Sally was a baby then. Tuck was purty sour for a while. He never said much, but we all figured he blamed himself for what happened.

"A year or so later the son and his wife died of typhoid fever. Soon as Tuck heard about it, he went over the pass to Fort Collins and fetched Sally back. She was little, just three or four, but Tuck raised her. He had a woman come in now and then, and later on some of the families in town kept her during the winter when she went to school, but Tuck can take most of the credit for Sally being what she is."

Veal reached for his pipe and tobacco, and added, "She's a damned fine girl."

The sheriff had told all of this for a purpose, Johnny thought, and he was irritated because it seemed to him that the purpose was to warn him. He said, "If I touch her, or harm her, or make her unhappy in any way, you'll come after me."

Veal tamped the tobacco into the bowl of his pipe, then looked up, grinning a little. "You put it mighty damned bald, but that's about the size of it. Here in the park we all kind of look out for each other, you might say, everybody but the Smelsers, that is. Now that Tuck's getting old, we try to do what we can for him, knowing he ain't gonna live much longer. If Sally ain't married by the time Tuck passes on, I guess we'll feel more responsible for her than ever."

"From what little I've seen of her," Johnny said, "she strikes me as a woman who can take care of herself."

"She's not a woman," Veal said. "She's a girl, and she needs looking after."

"How old is she?"

"Well, she's . . ." He started counting back on his fingers, and then laughed shortly. "She's twenty. Damned if I didn't think she was only sixteen. Shows how time gets the bulge on you."

"What does she think about the way everybody looks out for her?"

Veal puffed on his pipe for a moment, then he said: "You size things up purty good, Johnny. The truth is she gets a little sore about it, but mostly she's good-natured. She knows we're just trying to be helpful."

"I don't savvy yet why you don't like Highpockets Logan," Johnny said, feeling it was a question he could ask now.

"I just don't trust him," Veal said. "Not entirely, but I'll admit I'm prejudiced because I don't have nothing to go on. He's a hard worker and he appears to be loyal enough. I guess it's mostly that we all know he's in love with Sally and he's twice her age. We don't like it. None of us do."

"It occurs to me," Johnny said, "that it's a little queer you and Doc Rawls helped me get a job on the Double T. You don't know much about me."

"We both got a good impression," Veal said. "I don't know why. From the way you talk maybe, and the way you looked us in the eye. If you pan out the way we hope you will, maybe you and Sally will hit it off and we'd all be happy about it. But that's up to you and Sally. The main reason was that you went out of your way to save her and Tuck's life, even to risking your own, and that goes a hell of a long ways."

"The way I feel right now," Johnny said, "practically all women are bitches. I'm here because . . ." He paused and bit his lower lip, not wanting to talk about it or even think about it, then he went on: "Well, I told you why I'm here, so it ain't likely I'm going to do any falling in love. I need a job and I'll do my share of the work, and maybe stay through the winter. Chances are I'll be moving on in the spring."

"Not all women are bitches," Veal said. "My wife ain't. Sally ain't. Fact is, I know of only one woman in the park who flips her butt in your face so you know it's an invitation, and she don't get far. Not with most of us, I mean. I guess you'll always find some men who can't turn anything like that down."

Johnny nodded, thinking of Myrtle Allen and Dan Foley, then he said: "I'll get over it, I suppose. I'm not the first man who's had a woman make a fool out of him."

"That's right," Veal said. "I think all of us have been put through the wringer a time or two before we settled down."

"The first time I saw Sally," Johnny said thoughtfully, "I saw she was different from Linda. She's all business. You know, real direct. Kind of manlike."

"That's because she's been raised with men," Veal said. "But don't let that fool you. She's plenty of woman. My wife is a purty good judge of human nature, female nature anyway, and she says that Sally is the kind who will never jump into marriage, but when she does fall in love, it will be with everything she's got."

Later, with his head on his saddle, Johnny stared at the sky and thought that being married to Sally Tucker would be a very fine life indeed. Then, in spite of everything he could do, the scene with Linda at the time of Tom Tatum's death came into his mind like a killing frost, her spitting in his face, calling him a stupid fool in front of all those people, asking Sherm Balder to arrest him for the murder of Tom Tatum.

For a time he was physically sick as the memory with its violence and shame took possession of him, and he wondered if he could ever love another woman or even think of women in the way a man should.

They returned to the Double T late the following afternoon without finding the slightest trace of Wash Smelser. Sally asked Veal and Johnny to visit with her grandfather for just a moment. She said Doc Rawls thought he would make it, but he was very weak.

"Maybe we shouldn't see him for a while," Johnny said. "We'll tire him just talking to him."

Veal nodded. "I'll ride back out here in a day or two."

"No," Sally said. "Gramp made me promise to bring you in the minute you got back."

"All right," Veal said, "if you made a promise, you'll have to keep it."

Johnny followed Sally and Veal into the old man's bedroom. He looked very old and frail, his white beard and mustache and hair making the weathered skin of his face appear as sere as a last year's cotton-wood leaf, but his black eyes were sharp and clear. He held out a shaky hand to Johnny. "So you're the man who bought into a fight that wasn't your affair and saved Sally's hide along with mine."

"I figured it was the thing to do," Johnny said as he gripped the thin hand and released it to drop back on the quilt.

"A lot of men wouldn't have done it," the old man said. "I wanted to thank you. I don't care about myself because my time's about gone, but Sally's young with a whole life ahead of her. She says you're going to work for us."

"I need a job," Johnny said, "and she says you need a man."

"That's right," Tuck said. "We keep two men all year, but our winters are right out of the North Pole. You may find that feeding cattle in January ain't to your liking."

"I'll stay anyhow," Johnny said.

"Good." The old man's gaze turned to Veal. "Find Wash Smelser, Joe?"

"Not a trace," Veal said. "I've got a hunch he cleared out. Soon as I get back to town, I'll send word that he's wanted."

"He'll be back," the old man said.

Sally edged toward the door, making a surreptitious motion for them to follow her out of the room. Veal said, "I'll be back in a day or two to see you, Tuck," and left the room with Johnny and the girl.

While they were eating supper, Sally told them that Doc Rawls had found two men who would be out in the morning to finish haying, and Johnny would work with them. Highpockets Logan would have to tend the store until Tuck was out of danger. He took a great deal of attention and would continue to do so for the next two or three weeks according to the doctor.

That night Logan came into the bunkhouse as Johnny was pulling off his boots. He stood in the middle of the room beside the potbellied stove, his hands on his hips as he stared down at Johnny.

"We've got a couple of punkin rollers coming out tomorrow to wind up the haying," Logan said. "I don't want no trouble with you after they get here, so I'm gonna tell you something now. Stay away from Sally. Just because a saddle tramp rides by at the proper time don't give him no right to shine around her."

Johnny rose and picked his gun belt off the bunk and strapped it on. He stood there in his stocking feet, almost a head shorter than the long-legged Logan. He said: "Put on your gun, mister. We'll find out who's giving orders to who right now."

Logan backed up, his thin face turning pasty gray. "All right, all right," he said. "It ain't no cause of gun play."

He wheeled and walked to his bunk. Johnny remained standing, his gaze pinned on the tall man until he lay down with his back to Johnny. Joe Veal was right about him, but he was more than noise and bluster, Johnny thought. He was the kind who would be capable of shooting an enemy in the back, and as of this evening, Johnny Deere was an enemy.

— 15 —

Dan Foley sat in his hotel room staring at the man who stood beside the bureau. His name was Bob Kregg. At least that was the name Foley had heard in the saloons on Larimer Street. He had been in Denver more than a week. He had started making guarded inquiries, the name Bob Kregg had been given to him, and then he had checked references, men who knew how Kregg worked or could tell him about the job he had done in Brown's Hole or on some of the sheep-cattle battlegrounds of the western slope or on the Wyoming ranges where the word "homesteader" or "nester" was synonymous with rustler.

Now Foley wondered if Kregg was the man's real name. Perhaps he changed it from job to job and had to look in his hatband to see what he called himself at this particular time. In any case, Foley was fascinated in much the same way he would have been fascinated by the sleek, deadly figure of a mountain lion.

He had never seen a professional killer before and he had not been sure how he would react. He had supposed he'd be afraid because he had expected to see a big, rough-looking man, a bully type wearing two guns and a Bowie knife.

Bob Kregg was as opposite to this mental picture as anyone could be, and perhaps that was the reason he was not afraid. In fact, it was hard to believe that this man was a killer, that he could do what Foley wanted done, and for a time doubt was a strong negative power in his mind, so strong that he almost sent the man away.

Kregg was about thirty, Foley guessed. He was average size both in height and weight. He had a mustache that was exactly like a thousand other mustaches

Foley had seen since he had come to Denver. He wore an ordinary brown suit, a black derby, and polished cowboy boots, the only item of apparel which set him apart in the slightest way from the same thousand men who had grown identical mustaches.

He was not a talker, he was not a pusher, but above everything else, he was average, so average he was almost faceless, the kind of man Foley would have passed on the street or seen in a crowd at the Union Station without being aware he was there. Or, if for any reason he'd had his attention called to the man, he would never have been able to describe him, or even identify him if he had been asked to do so a short time later.

Apparently Kregg was used to being stared at by prospective employers. He looked past Foley at the window as if oblivious to his presence, his face expressionless; he seemed perfectly at ease and he had nothing to say unless he was spoken to. Without opening his mouth, he was making it plain that the next move was up to Foley who could hire him or send him on his way and there would be no hard feelings or anything said.

Foley rose, suddenly feeling an attack of jitters. He was not as cold-blooded about this business as he had thought he would be. Johnny Deere's high-boned, youthful face appeared in front of him then, and Foley saw him lying dead on the street of some town, whatever town they had in North Park. He walked to the bureau and, picking up a box of cigars, offered one to Kregg who shook his head.

"I don't smoke," he said.

Foley opened the top drawer and took out a whiskey bottle. He poured a stiff drink into a glass and held it out to Kregg.

"I don't drink," Kregg said.

Foley turned and walked slowly to the window, his back to Kregg. The man didn't have a nerve in his body or a drop of human blood in his veins. He was a machine. If Foley had been able to offer a beautiful woman, Kregg would undoubtedly have said in that same neutral voice, "I don't need a woman." He had no sins, this Bob Kregg. All he did was to hire out to kill men.

Foley downed the drink and turned to catch a faint hint of amusement in the man's gray eyes. He said, "You come highly recommended."

Kregg nodded as if he knew that. "I do good work."

"I'll pay five hundred dollars now and a second five hundred when the job is finished."

"That's satisfactory," Kregg said. "It's the way I'm usually paid." He paused and added, "I always am paid, Foley."

It was not a threat; it was a simple statement of fact. Foley said quickly, "You'll get your money. Here's the first five hundred now." He handed a buckskin bag to

Kregg. "I want you to understand that this is not my deal. I'm only the middleman. You're working for old Bull Tatum who owns a big spread north of Star City."

"I've heard of him," Kregg said. "His outfit's Rainbow, isn't it?"

"That's right," Foley said. "His son was killed in a brawl at a dance in Star City. The man who used the knife is named Johnny Deere. Old Bull wants him punished because the law didn't touch him."

"I understand," Kregg said.

"He's in North Park and I expect him to stay there for a while," Foley said. "I don't know what outfit he's working for, but you won't have any trouble finding him. He's not the kind who will change his name. As soon as I hear from you that you've earned the balance of your money, I'll come to Denver. You can find me in this hotel."

"All right," Kregg said. "That all?"

"One more thing. Old Bull wants him to know why he's getting it."

Kregg nodded and turned to the door. "How will you go at this?" Foley asked.

Kregg swung back and stood staring at Foley, the hint of amusement in his eyes again. "I work quick and I work clean. You'll hear from me in a few days. My letter will state that the shipment of beef is on its way to Denver and you will be able to contact me on such and such a date when I will expect to be paid for services rendered."

Kregg turned and opened the door. "I asked you how you . . ." Foley began. But Kregg was gone and Dan Foley was staring at the closed door.

He cursed aloud and, going to the bureau, picked up the bottle and poured another drink. He had never, he told himself, met as cold-blooded a bastard in his life as this Bob Kregg or whatever his name was. Now he did not have the slightest doubt about the killer fulfilling his contract.

He took a night train to Sterling, ate breakfast, and rode out of town, arriving in Star City late in the afternoon. He turned his horse over to Al Frolich in the livery stable and went at once to the courthouse where he found Sherm Balder in his office. For a moment the sheriff stared at him, his mouth firming into an expression of distaste before he turned to his desk and, opening a drawer, took out a star and tossed it to Foley.

"Thanks, Sherm." Foley held the badge in his hand and stared at it. "I thought you'd change your mind."

"By God, Dan," Sherm cried out in a voice that was filled with misery, "have you gone daft?"

"No," Foley answered. "Let's say I've gained some sense. It's quite a trick after living for twenty-three years in this country without knowing how to do anything, but I know now."

"You've gained something, all right," Sherm said

bitterly, "but I ain't sure it's sense. I'm resigning the first of the year and I understand you'll be appointed sheriff."

"That's the plan," Foley said blandly, still staring at the shiny badge in his hand. "Are these things really tin like they say, Sherm?"

"No, it's silver, and don't you forget it if you're going to wear it." Sherm took a ragged breath, then demanded, "What changed you, Dan? It started the night Tom Tatum was killed. I've thought about it a thousand times since then. You started taking over. You never had before."

"No, I never had before." Foley pinned the star to his vest and looked at it with pride, then lifted his head to meet Sherm Balder's gaze. "Sherm, you're going to be sorry as long as you live that you helped run Johnny out of town the night Tom Tatum was killed."

"But you helped, too."

"Sure I did," Foley admitted. "It went exactly the way I planned and it was only the beginning. It didn't start that night, Sherm. It started a long time before when I began noticing the way folks looked at me and treated me, and the different way they looked at Johnny and treated him." He turned to the door, calling back, "I'll take care of things Saturday night, Sherm. You've been letting the boys get out of hand a little."

He strode along the street toward the Hollison

house, deciding that he would see Linda today, sick or well. He had put it off too long because her mother had promised to tell him when she was able to see him. Now, thinking about it, it occurred to him that Mrs. Hollison didn't want him to see Linda. If that were the case, he had better take charge of this situation, too.

Now that it was late September, the days were cooler and Linda should be feeling better, he thought. He wondered for a moment how she had really felt about Johnny Deere. Oh, she'd hated him the night Tom was killed. No doubt about that.

In a matter of seconds Johnny had destroyed all of her fine planning, so it was natural enough for her to hate him, but he'd read somewhere that hate and love were not far apart. He had a feeling that she had loved Johnny without even knowing it herself. He would find out if it were true. If so, she would be punished just as old Bull wanted her to be. There was one thing about which he was sure. She had never loved Tom Tatum.

He strode rapidly along the path from the street and, stepping up on the porch, yanked on the bellpull. He waited and gave it a second tug before she opened the door. She said, "Oh, I didn't expect you, Dan. Come in."

For a moment he stood staring at her, thinking that she had already been punished in a way that old Bull would find satisfactory. She was very pale, and that was astonishing because even as a little girl she'd had a cherry-cheeked appearance that was one of her most attractive features. She had lost weight, too, so that the roundness of her figure that he had admired so much was gone.

"I've been aiming to call," he said, "but your mother said you weren't well."

"I've been well enough," she said. "I just haven't felt like doing anything or going anywhere," She stepped back. "Come in. It will be nice to have someone to talk to."

He followed her into the front room and sat down beside her on the black leather couch. He said, "You're pale, Linda. You've been in the house too much. I'll get a buggy from Al Frolich Sunday and take you for a ride. Would you like that?"

"I'd love it," she said listlessly. "I haven't seen you since the day of Tom's funeral. I've been wanting to thank you for standing up to old Bull. You're the only man in town who would have done it. Ever since that day I've thought how much I had misjudged you."

"Yes," he said somberly, "you and everyone else." He touched the star on his vest. "I'm a deputy now. After Sherm retires, I'll run for sheriff. A few months ago I wouldn't even have thought of doing anything like that."

She was surprised and interested, and for a moment

he sensed that she had her old vitality and spark that had set her apart from all the other girls he had ever known. She said, "No, I guess you wouldn't. Now that you're deputy, you'll arrest Johnny Deere if he ever comes back, won't you?"

"Of course I will," he said, "but he won't come back. Besides, he'll be punished in one way or another."

"He's got to be, Dan," she said. "He's got to be."

"Listen to me, Linda," he said. "You've got to forget Johnny. Tom, too. I mean, you can't live for someone who's dead."

"I know," she said, listless again.

"I love you, Linda," he said softly, "and I want to marry you, but I won't rush you, partly because I want you to think about it and try to forget what's happened, and partly because I'm going to be an important man in this country and I'll be able to support you the way you deserve to be supported. I want to get started so you'll know I'm not just bragging."

Again he saw the spark of the old Linda. She didn't laugh at him as she had once when he had asked her to marry him. She was thinking about his father and the ranch above town, and that when his father died, he would receive part of the property. He wouldn't tell her that he was going to make it himself and in his own way, and that old Bull Tatum and not Rip Foley was the goose who would fill Dan Foley's nest with gold eggs.

She smiled. "It will be a nice thing to think about, Dan."

He left a few minutes later, saying he would be by for her about two Sunday afternoon. As he walked back toward the hotel where he planned to take a room, he wondered how much he could push her. If he had his way, they would be married tomorrow, but he couldn't afford to run the risk of failure.

He wished that before Johnny Deere died with Bob Kregg's bullet in his heart he could be told that Dan Foley was going to marry Linda Hollison. And he was, he told himself. The only question was one of time.

— 1 6 —

Soon after haying, an early storm laid a heavy coat of snow on the tall peaks of the Medicine Bows and started the cattle drifting down to the lower elevation of the park floor. Johnny rode roundup with the Double T's neighbors, the Bartons and the Zacharys and others, men he had not met but who seemed to know about him.

Tuck was recovering his strength slowly and was up only a few minutes each day, so Sally was kept busy with housework and the care of the old man. Highpockets Logan stayed at the Double T to look after the store and do the necessary chores, and

Johnny rode north with the pool herd to the railroad at Laramie.

When he returned with the other park ranchers, he stopped at the Barton ranch for dinner. Mrs. Barton gave him a note that Joe Veal had left with her two days ago. "He waited for you till dark," she told him. "I said I thought you men would be back that day." She glared at her husband. "I suppose you got on a toot and couldn't get out of Laramie."

"We did not," Barton snapped. "We had to wait for cars and we were in Laramie with cattle two days longer than we figured."

Johnny moved to the window and unfolded the paper. He read, "Dear Johnny, I want you to come to town immediately and get hold of me before you see anyone else. Do not go on to the Double T first. Joe. P.S. Damn it, boy, this is important. Do what I'm telling you."

Johnny wadded up the note and jammed it into his pocket. "Joe wants me to come to town and see him before I go to the Double T. He didn't say why."

Mrs. Barton shook her head. "He's close-mouthed, Joe is. He said for me to be sure you got this if I had to run a mile behind you before I caught up with you." She motioned to the table. "Sit down, both of you, though I don't know if Marvin deserves anything from me or not. I don't believe that yarn about having to wait for cars. You ain't married, Johnny, so it's all right for you to go on a toot, but Marvin's got kids and he's got me, though many's the time I wonder how he done it. I say it ain't right for him to blow a lot of money on whiskey and . . . and fast women."

"Oh, for God's sake, Effie," Barton said. "If you've got to call me a liar, do it after Johnny's gone."

"I will," she said. "I'm just working up to a good start." She turned to Johnny. "How about it? Was he lying?"

"He sure wasn't," Johnny said.

"Oh, you men all hang together," she said, but she seemed mollified.

When he finished eating and rose to go, she said, "We're having a dance here Saturday night, seeing as we've got the biggest house on this side of the park. Do you think you could bring Sally? I sure don't like for her to have that Highpockets Logan fetching her and her being out with him after dark. I wish Tuck would fire him."

"I'll be glad to bring her," Johnny said, "if she'll come with me."

"She'll come, all right," Mrs. Barton said. "Just tell her I asked you to fetch her. Shucks, you don't have to even say that. Just ask her."

"I will," he said. "Thanks for the dinner."

"You're more'n welcome," she said, "though I can't say as much for some men who ain't more'n ten feet away from where I'm sitting."

She was smiling now and Johnny decided the worst of the family storm was over. He said, "You may be sleeping in the barn tonight, Marvin."

"Sounds like it," Barton said ruefully, "and all on account of the damned railroad."

"He'd be sleeping in the barn, railroad or no railroad," Mrs. Barton said, "but my feet have been cold ever since he left."

"So I'll get 'em right in the middle of my back," Barton said.

On the way to town Johnny pondered the meaning of the sheriff's note, but he could not think of anything that seemed logical. Then he thought about Mrs. Barton's invitation to the dance and her suggestion that he bring Sally. Taken alone it wasn't so strange, but the part about not wanting Sally to be out in the dark with Logan was very strange.

He had been accepted immediately by the people of the park and that was very gratifying. He had learned during the roundup and the drive to Laramie that Joe Veal was highly respected and that he was a sort of barometer of public opinion. He wasn't sure which was cause and which was effect. Perhaps the sheriff put his finger to the wind and thought what most of the people thought but Johnny was inclined to think it worked the other way, that people thought what Joe Veal thought.

A wind sprang up before Johnny reached town, carrying clouds of dust along the park floor. Another storm was on the way, he decided, as he tied in front of the courthouse and went in.

Joe Veal jumped out of his chair the instant he saw Johnny. He shouted, "By God, boy, I'm glad to see you!" He shook Johnny's hand and motioned toward a chair. "Just now get in?"

Johnny nodded. "Mrs. Barton gave me your note."

"Good." Veal walked nervously around his desk. "Did you ever hear of a man named Bob Kregg?"

Johnny thought a moment, then shook his head. "Not that I can remember."

"Well, there's a man in town who calls himself Bob Kregg. He says he's here to kill you."

Johnny rose. "Where is he?"

"Sit down, damn it. Sit down." When Johnny obeyed, Veal said, "Now there's no reason for you to go off half-cocked. This hairpin rode in on the stage from Laramie while you were on roundup. He got a hotel room and bought a horse and began riding around, then he started asking for you. I told folks to keep their mouths shut. All of 'em did but High-pockets Logan. He was in the Top Notch Saloon one night when Kregg was asking, so he told him.

"The next day Kregg rode out to the Double T looking for you. Sally said you was gone. Then Kregg told her a yarn about how you'd wronged his sister in Star City and he was here to kill you on account of what you'd done."

Johnny rose and checked his revolver. "Where is he, Joe? If you don't tell me, I've got to start hunting."

"No you don't," Veal shouted angrily. "I told you not to go off half-cocked. Sally didn't believe it. Nobody believes it but Highpockets Logan. Folks have been giving Kregg the cold shoulder. Now he's a fast-draw man. A hired killer if I ever seen one. This dodge about a sister being wronged is an old one. Usually it works because it puts public opinion on the side of the killer if his victim is a stranger like you, but it didn't work here because I told everybody the real reason you left Star City. Now if you'll . . ."

"How do you know I didn't lie to you?"

Veal hesitated, turned red in the face, and then he said, "If you've got to know, I'll tell you. I believed you when you first got here, but with you working for Sally, I didn't want to take no chances, so I wrote to Sherm Balder and he wrote the same story you'd told me. Now if you'll just ride out of town for a while, we'll figure out a way to get rid . . ."

Johnny turned to the door and walked out of the sheriff's office. Veal yelled, "What the hell are you gonna do?"

Johnny turned to face him. "I'm going to hunt this Kregg up."

"You can't do it," Veal said in exasperation. "He'll kill you. You're a working cowhand. He's a gunslinger. Did you ever pull a gun on a man?"

"No. Not like this is gonna be."

"Well, he has. You can count on it. I've seen his kind before. It'll take you two or three seconds to draw and fire and hit anything. By that time he'll have his gun empty and chances are he'll have three, maybe four of the five slugs in your heart."

"It's a chance I've got to take," Johnny said. "If I ride out of town I've got to keep on riding. We both know it, so what are you arguing about?"

Veal swallowed, fighting his anger and anxiety, then he held out his hand. "Good luck, boy."

"Thanks." Johnny shook his hand, warmed by the thought that he had made more friends in the short time he'd been in North Park than he'd made in all the years he'd lived in the Pole Creek country. "Where is he?"

"In the Top Notch."

"Tell him I'll be at the hotel waiting for him, and he'd better come shooting."

"I'll tell him." Veal hesitated, then wheeled and strode out of the courthouse.

Johnny waited until the sheriff was halfway to the Top Notch Saloon which was across the street and at the other end of the block from the hotel. He walked to his horse, pulled his Winchester from the boot, and strode quickly to the hotel. There he leaned his rifle against the wall and stood watching the door of the Top Notch.

A hard gust of wind picked up a cloud of dust from the street. Johnny turned his head and shut his eyes until the dust swept by. The wind was steady and piercing, rattling the signs and awnings along the street. He could make allowances for it, but the sharp gusts which hit hard and unexpectedly were another matter. The wind kept people off the street and that was one thing for which he was thankful.

He had no idea of time, but it took longer for Kregg to get into the street than Johnny had expected. At first he had not been afraid because this was something he had anticipated from the time he had first come to the park and he had gone over in his mind exactly what he would do. Now, with the seconds ticking away, he felt his nerves tighten until he realized that this was what Bob Kregg wanted. After that it was better because it showed him that even a professional was not above feeling fear at a time like this.

A man stepped into the street from the Top Notch, an average-size man in a brown suit. He had a gun belt strapped around his waist, the holster tied down, but aside from that, he might have been an ordinary drummer. Even the derby hat added to the illusion.

"Are you Kregg?" Johnny yelled.

"I'm Kregg," the man shouted back. "I'm here to kill you, you son of a . . ."

He never finished. Johnny drew his gun and started shooting. Kregg let out a high yell and bawled something about Johnny being a damned fool, but Johnny kept on shooting. Kregg ran toward him, his revolver in his hand. The distance was too great for a pistol, and Johnny knew it as well as Kregg did. His bullets were wide, kicking up dust on one side of Kregg and then the other, with one striking far in front of him.

When the last shell had been fired, Johnny tossed the pistol into the street and, wheeling to his Winchester, picked it up and dropped to one knee. He thumbed back the hammer as Kregg fired in desperation. Johnny began shooting as Kregg's bullets dug into the street dust. His first shot was a miss, the second a hit that stopped the running Kregg as suddenly as if he had run headlong into the side of a building. He pulled the trigger of his revolver one more time, the bullet driving into the ground a few feet in front of him, and then he went down.

Johnny paced toward him, holding the Winchester on the ready as he watched Kregg raise himself up on his knees, the gun still clutched in his right hand. Blood bubbled at the corners of his mouth and ran down his chin as he tried to bring his revolver up, but the strength had drained out of him. He toppled forward on his face, his hat coming off and rolling and turning with its crown pointed at the sky. His fingers went slack and slipped off the walnut butt of his gun.

Men ran out of the buildings along the street. He didn't know most of them, but he shook hands and listened to their congratulations. When Veal came to him, he asked, "You going to hold me?"

"Hell no," the sheriff said. "You went coyote hunting and you nailed one."

Doc Rawls had knelt beside Kregg. Now he rose and nodded at Johnny. "An excellent shot for a man under fire." Then, looking past the bulky figure of the medico, Johnny saw Highpockets Logan stride toward the livery stable.

"I'll be riding," Johnny said.

It was dark by the time he reached the Double T. He was cold and tired, and in a somber mood as a result of the shooting, so he was relieved when a man loomed before him, asking, "You Johnny Deere?"

"That's right."

"My name's Tug Randall," the man said. "They hired me just after you started for Laramie. Miss Sally, she said to take care of your horse for you if you got here before I went to bed. You go on in. She'll have something for you to eat."

"Thanks," Johnny said. "It's been a long day."

The first flakes of snow stung his face as he crossed the yard to the back door. When he went in, Sally was stirring something on the stove. She cried out when she saw him and ran to him, her eyes radiant.

"Johnny, I'm glad you're back." She gripped his arms and looked up at him. "There's a man in town who's looking for you."

"He was aiming to kill me," Johnny said, "but they'll be burying him instead. I heard about him when I got to Barton's. Joe Veal had left a note for me."

"I'm glad," she said. "These last days have been awful. I was afraid he'd find you before you heard about him."

He reached out as she turned away and brought her around to face him. It was the first time that she had seemed entirely feminine, the first time she had thrown aside the cloak of efficiency which she wore so well. Now, seeing her this way, he knew that he loved her, that any feeling he'd had for Linda Hollison had been superficial. Knowing that, he realized he would never be plagued by it again.

"Sally, do you have any idea how good it is to be back and to know you've been concerned about me?" He put his arms around her and held her against him for a moment, strongly tempted to tell her how he felt, tell her that he wanted to stay here and take care of her, to live in the park with her friends who were becoming his friends, but he could not. He was a walking dead man. Old Bull Tatum would try again and again. Sometime he would succeed.

He let her go, saying, "A fellow who took my horse said you'd have something for me to eat."

"Right away," she said, and turned to the stove. "I hired Tug Randall about the time you left for Laramie."

"Where's Highpockets?"

"I don't have the slightest idea," she said him. You see, he was the one who told Kregg were working here."

"Joe didn't like Highpockets," he said. "I'll bet he was glad to see you let him go."

"I know," she said. "Joe thought I should have let him go a long time ago, but I never had a real good reason before."

"Mrs. Barton didn't know," he said. "She wants me to bring you to a dance over there Saturday night. She didn't want you out in the dark with Highpockets."

She was the usual efficient, straightforward Sally now, completely self-controlled. "No, I didn't tell her. I get a little tired of everybody in the park including Joe Veal trying to take care of me. I can go alone. You don't have to bother."

"I'd like to take you," he said, "unless you don't want to be seen with your hired help."

"Don't be a fool," she flared. "Of course I want to be seen with you. After what you did for Grandpa and me, you're not just hired help."

"Then we'll figure on it," he said.

He sat down at the table and watched her fix his supper. She was disappointed, he knew, for she had been ready to be told that he loved her, but he couldn't. Someday, he told himself, he would tell her why.

By the end of the year Dan Foley was established in the minds of the Pole Creek folks as the sheriff. So, when Sherm Balder resigned, Foley was appointed to take his place. No one was surprised and no one laughed.

The surprise and laughter had come weeks ago when he first pinned the star to his vest. Neither had lasted very long. In fact, they had not lasted after the first Saturday night. Foley had gone from one saloon to another, he had stopped fights as soon as they started by cracking a few heads together, and had thrown three cowhands into jail and kept them there until they were tried Monday morning for disturbing the peace.

Everybody, and that included Rip Foley and his two oldest sons, scratched their heads and asked what had come over easygoing, comical Dan Foley. Rip even rode into town Monday and told Dan his mother was worried about him and would he please move back home. Foley said no, he had a job to do and he aimed to do it, so Rip rode home, still scratching his head and finding it hard to see in this tough and stubborn man the baby boy that he and his wife had mentally pictured for twenty-three years.

Dakota Sam Weeks put it very well in his editorial

in the next week's issue of the *Star City Clarion:* "Star City has not known any serious crime for years, but there has been a growing spirit of boisterous horseplay on Saturday nights, particularly in the saloons and at the family dances in the Oddfellows Hall. We are not forgetting the dignity and honesty with which Sherm Balder has clothed the sheriffs office, but we are also remembering that age has crept up on Sherm so that he moves more slowly than he did at one time and his vision is not as clear as it once was. The result has been that when a fight broke out, Sherm was too slow getting there to stop it, or he didn't see it at all.

"We all remember the unfortunate death of Tom Tatum at a recent Saturday night dance. It could have been prevented and it should have been. Now that the horse has been stolen, our worthy Sheriff is closing and locking the barn door by appointing Dan Foley deputy. We applaud this belated action and we have every reason to believe that from now on Saturday nights in Star City will be quiet and orderly.

"However, there is one question which not even our worthy neighbor, Rip Foley, is able to answer. What happened to his youngest son who was a tiger wearing a star last Saturday night, Dan Foley the erstwhile Pole Creek clown? We accused Rip of feeding his son copious quantities of raw beefsteak butchered from the wildest steers on the Foley range, but Rip vociferously denies the charge in his usual stentorian voice."

Even old Bull Tatum grudgingly admitted that maybe Dan Foley would do, and that it was a good thing for Rainbow to have a Tatum man in the sheriff's office. Then he demanded: "What the hell happened to you, son? I never knowed a pet dog to turn a wolf overnight."

"It wasn't overnight, Mr. Tatum," Foley said. "It's been happening a long time. A man can stand some things for quite a spell, and then all of a sudden he can't stand it no longer and he boils over. I boiled over the night Tom was killed."

Old Bull stared through the window at the rolling prairie for a long time. Finally he nodded and allowed he could understand what had happened to Foley, that he hadn't been any great shakes until he'd moved onto the hard land north of Pole Creek and started Rainbow. Then he asked, "What about Johnny Deere?"

"He's been taken care of," Foley said.

"The girl?"

Foley gave him a thin-lipped smile. "I hope you understand this, Mr. Tatum. I aim to marry her. I promise you that she'll be punished."

Tatum nodded, understanding exactly what Foley meant. In his opinion, a man like Slow Sam was a better cook and housekeeper than any woman. To him a woman had only one use, and as far as he was concerned, marriage was an institution designed to legalize that use.

"What about Frank Deere?" Tatum asked.

"That will take a little time," Foley answered, and old Bull didn't press him.

In spite of his definite assurance to old Bull that Johnny Deere had been taken care of, Foley had a steadily increasing doubt as the weeks passed and he had no word from Bob Kregg. The man said he worked quick and clean, and that Foley would get a letter from him saying the beef shipment had been made and he could be contacted at a certain time in Denver, but no such letter had come.

Foley had no idea why the gunman wasn't calling for the balance of his money, but any thought that he might have failed was ridiculous. When he mentally pictured the cold-eyed man he had hired in his Denver hotel room, it became more than ridiculous. He did know one thing. He had to tell old Bull that Johnny Deere was dead.

He had taken the money and now, if by any chance something had gone wrong, if Kregg, for instance, had pocketed the fee Foley had given him and left the country, there was nothing for Foley to do but hire another man. If it cost more than the $500 he had left, he would have to put up the balance of the money himself.

After Sherm Balder moved out of the Sheriff's office, Foley thumbed through the official correspondence that Sherm had left along with a stack of reward dodgers. One of the latter pictured a young, thin-faced man named Wash Smelser who was wanted in North Park for the attempted robbery and murder of a rancher named Tuck Tucker.

Later, while reading through the correspondence, he received a jolt when he found a letter from the sheriff in North Park named Joe Veal who asked if Johnny Deere was wanted by the law and why he had left the Pole Creek country.

Foley swore as he crumpled the letter and threw it into the stove. Sherm would have been fool enough to have told the truth, so if Bob Kregg had ridden into North Park with some cock-and-bull story about Johnny being wanted by the law and he was a bounty hunter, he might have been tossed into jail.

That, Foley decided, was the reason he had not heard from Kregg who might have to stay in the park all winter, but after all this time he was certainly out of jail and had completed his contract. Foley would likely hear from him as soon as the weather broke in the spring.

Early in February Foley received a second letter from Johnny. Foley had never answered the first one, thinking that it wouldn't be necessary since Johnny didn't have long to live, but now he realized he had made a serious mistake. The letter was dated about a month before so it either had not been mailed for some time or the mail stage had been held up by bad weather. In any case, Johnny was very much alive as of January third when he had written the letter.

Foley scanned the page, noting nothing of importance beyond the news that Johnny had a job working on the Double T, a fair-sized spread owned by an old man named Tuck Tucker. Everything was fine except that Johnny wondered why he hadn't heard from Foley and asked about his father. He would be writing directly to his father if he didn't hear from Foley soon.

When Foley reached the last paragraph, he received an even bigger jolt than when he had found the letter from Joe Veal. Johnny said that last fall a gunslinger named Bob Kregg had been hired by old Bull Tatum to get him ready for burying, but instead, Kregg was the one who got ready for burying.

For a time Foley was a madman. He paced around the office cursing Johnny and Bob Kregg and the United States mail. He took a bottle out of his desk and drank, but it didn't help. Nothing helped because this was impossible. It simply could not have happened. For Johnny Deere to have gunned down a professional killer like Bob Kregg was as completely unreasonable as to say that Pole Creek was flowing west instead of east.

He took his horse from Al Frolich's livery stable and rode into the sand hills, reason slowly returning to him. Johnny had changed and he might as well face it.

Foley had changed, too, or at least folks thought he had. Actually it wasn't a change at all; he was the same man he had been six months ago. The only difference was that the opportunity he had been waiting for had finally come his way.

Well, it wasn't exactly opportunity that had come Johnny's way, but circumstances had forced him to change. He had killed Tom Tatum by accident, then he had been forced to kill Jess Crowder who would have killed him if he hadn't, and now, through some crazy twist of circumstances, he had got the drop on Bob Kregg and killed him. He couldn't go on riding his good luck forever. Next time it would be different. Whatever happened, he must not be allowed to come back. There was nothing to bring him except his father, so it was necessary to remove the old man.

He reined up in front of the Deere sod house and tied; then, with his gun dangling in his right hand at his side, he knocked on the door. Frank recognized Foley as soon as he opened the door and smiled. "Come in, Dan. Have you heard from Johnny?"

He was old and thin, with the sadness of defeat stamped upon his wrinkled face. Just for an instant his eyes were bright and eager, his liver-brown lips parted as he waited for Foley to answer, but Foley didn't bother. He raised his gun and shot the old man through the head, feeling a hysterical urge to laugh as he saw the expression of surprise and alarm come into Frank

Deere's face, then fade in the slackness of death.

Foley stepped inside and holstered the gun. He searched for a pistol, hoping he could make it look like suicide, but the only gun of any kind in the house was a shotgun. He fired into the old man's face, disfiguring it so much that the chances were Doc Allen would never discover the revolver bullet.

He removed the dead man's right shoe and sock so it would seem that he might have fired the shotgun with the big toe of his right foot. He left the shotgun beside the body, stepped outside and mounted. No one was in sight. He rode away, thankful that the usual wind was blowing so that the hoof tracks in the sand of the road would soon be obliterated.

He returned to town from the east, stopped at the Hollison house for a few minutes to talk to Linda, and went on to the livery stable. Linda had promised to marry him and he thought it would be soon, although he felt the pressure of Mrs. Hollison's opposition. Linda had always been headstrong and had found means of getting her way, so Foley did not doubt that Linda, who was eighteen now, would soon be having her way again and would set the date.

He wrote a letter to Johnny, saying he had just been out to talk to his father, and he was well and glad to learn that Johnny was doing so well. Foley hesitated, then added that he was happy to learn that it wasn't Johnny who had been buried.

He rode to Sterling the next day and mailed the letter, not wanting anyone in Star City to know that he had written to Johnny. The two letters he had received had not had Johnny's name or return address on the outside of the envelope.

Two days later Benny Quinn brought Frank Deere's body in. Doc Allen, functioning as coroner, called it suicide. Everyone except old Bull Tatum and the Rainbow crew went to the funeral, and the old-timers, Sherm Balder in particular, wept unashamedly because Frank Deere had been one of the town founders and deserved a better life than he'd had.

Dan Foley was there, too, apparently grieving as much as the others. After the funeral he asked Sherm Balder what would be done with the estate. There were a few head of cattle, two horses, and some chickens and pigs to dispose of.

The quarter section of land wasn't worth much, but Benny Quinn would probably buy it. He didn't have any money, but they could give as much time as he needed. He'd be good for it eventually. Only thing was, Sherm said, nobody knew where Johnny was. They'd have to bank the money and hold it until he returned or let someone know where he was.

Foley said he sure didn't know. Later when he was back in his office he thought about the letter Sherm had received from Joe Veal last fall. It would be easy enough for Sherm to write to Veal and find out where

Johnny was. At least Veal would know whether Johnny was still in North Park. Maybe Sherm had forgotten about it, so Foley decided to let it ride.

The letter was destroyed. Unless Sherm remembered it, or unless Johnny wrote to someone else, he would not know about his father. There would be no problem in a few weeks when the weather broke and Foley got another man up there. Johnny wouldn't be knowing anything.

— 1 8 —

The winter in North Park was a hard one. Storm followed storm, with clear, cold days between, the temperature staying close to zero or below. Johnny had not expected weather like this. Still, he had no regrets. Tug Randall was an easy man to work with. They had an ample supply of hay to get through the winter. Tuck was better, so Sally was able to leave him alone most of the time while she did the housework or ran over to the store if a customer drove up.

Even with the excessive amount of feeding that had to be done to keep the cattle alive, the park ranchers found time for pie or basket socials at the school or dances in their homes, usually the Barton place which had the biggest front room of any of the ranch houses on the eastern side of the park.

Johnny took Sally to all the social events, and when the weather wasn't too bad, they bundled Tuck up with buffalo robes and placed a hot iron at his feet and took off in the sleigh. Usually he had a good time, although Sally and Johnny always had to leave early to get Tuck back home and in bed before he gave out.

Johnny often had a terrifying feeling that his life on the Double T was too good to last. He liked and respected Tuck, and spent most of the few leisure hours that he had playing checkers with the old man, or cards when Sally or Tug Randall had time to sit in on the game.

As far as his relationship with Sally was concerned, it was an idyllic situation which would have been perfect if he had felt free to ask her to marry him. More and more he sensed that her cloak of competence and self-assurance was slipping from her; he felt it in the way she looked at him when she thought he wasn't aware of it, the smiles she gave him, the things she went out of her way to do for him.

Sometimes he had a feeling she was going to tell him she loved him. He would not have minded if she had, but she never did. Then, for some unaccountable reason, a strange tension developed between them. He sensed it early in March. As the month dragged by it grew worse.

He felt that he could not change anything in their relationship, but he realized by the end of March that something had to change, that they could not go on living this way, yet at the same time he could not walk off. Competent help was hard to get and Tug Randall could not handle the work by himself. More than that, spring was at hand with its tailing up and bog riding and calving, and they would be even busier than they were now.

The bubble broke on the night of April first in a totally unexpected manner. Johnny was responsible for it, although he had not intended it to work that way. They had taken Tuck in the hack to Barton's for an April Fool party. A chinook had taken the snow off and left the road a loblolly which made travel difficult.

They had to bring Tuck back shortly after midnight before the refreshments were served. Johnny pulled the hack in as close to the front door as he could and helped Tuck into the house. When he returned from putting the horses away, Tuck was in bed and Sally had built a fire in the kitchen and had put a pot of coffee on the stove.

When she heard the front door close, she called, "Johnny, will you start a fire in the fireplace? I'm making coffee and we have some of the cake left from supper. I thought we'd have our own party."

"Sounds good," he said. "I'm hungry."

He used enough pitch pine to start a quick fire, then went into the kitchen. She had cut liberal slices of cake and had moved them from the pan to plates. She was standing by the range waiting for the coffee. She glanced over her shoulder and smiled as she said, "Patience. It will be ready in a minute."

"I've got all the patience in the world," he said.

"I believe you have," she agreed.

For a time he stood looking down at the top of her head and the back of her neck. She was wearing a red dress that he thought was silk from the way it rustled. He sensed that it was new and wondered how she had found time to work on it. Although the dress covered the round softness of her body, it made him aware of it, too, and impulsively he bent and kissed her on the back of her neck.

She cried out and whirled to face him, her arms going out to him. "Johnny, did you . . ." She stopped and could not go on, and stood that way, her full lips parted, waiting.

"I've tried to keep from touching you," he said. "I'm sorry I did that."

"Why are you sorry?" she asked. "And why have you tried to keep from touching me?"

"It's a long story." He knew then that he had to tell her, and added, "When the coffee's hot, I will tell you." He reached out and took her into his arms. "No use wasting time while we wait, is there?"

"No use at all," she said.

He kissed her and she clung to him fiercely, and at the same time he found her lips so sweet and so yielding that he felt as if he were being swept away on a wave that was the very force of life itself. He knew then that he had been a fool to wait, that happiness should be taken when and where it could be taken. Happiness was transient at best, and even now he knew that he might have waited too long.

When she drew her lips from his, she raised her hands to his cheeks and caressed them as she asked, "Johnny, Johnny, why have you never done that before?"

"I've wanted to for a long time," he said. "I've loved you since that night when I got back from Laramie and found out that you were worried about me. I've discovered a new life here. It's been a good life, as good as a man could ever ask for, and I couldn't risk ruining yours by making you a widow in a few weeks or months."

"If you meant that Bob Kregg who came here with that silly story . . ."

"No, it wasn't that." He shook his head. "You and Joe Veal and I guess almost everybody knew it was a lie." He paused, and then asked, "Is the coffee ready?"

"It's ready," she said. "Let's sit in front of the fireplace. You take the cake and I'll bring the coffee."

He started talking as soon as they sat down. He told her everything, even the humiliating details of how Linda Hollison had tried to use him. He said, "That was a little more than seven months ago, but it seems like seven years. I'm that much older now. I was wrong to leave. If I had it to do over, I'd have stayed." He shrugged. "But that would have been wrong, too. I wouldn't have met you."

"I'd be dead and so would Grandpa," she said. "Now will you eat your cake? I'll pour the coffee back into the pot and give you a hot cup."

She had not been surprised, he thought, and wondered if Joe Veal had told her. Later, after he finished eating and had thrown more wood on the fire, she sat beside him, his arm around her. "You should have told me all this before," she said. "It would have been much worse if you had been killed without ever telling me you loved me. You don't know how much I wanted to hear you say that and have you kiss me."

"But we couldn't get married," he said. "It wouldn't be right. This is what I'm trying to say. Tatum will never let me rest. I've killed three men. Two of them were his men who were trying to kill me. Next time it may be a dry gulcher who will shoot me from the brush. If it was just me, well, that's one thing, but if I've got to think of you and maybe a baby, I . . . I just couldn't stand it."

"Oh, you're wrong, Johnny," she whispered. "So terribly wrong. I've read novels about men going off to war and being noble and telling their sweethearts they'll wait until the war's over. That's not the way a woman wants it. I'd rather have you for a little while than never to have you at all. I've taken care of myself for a long time, with the help of everyone in North Park, of course. If there is a baby, I can take care of him, too."

He was silent a long time, knowing what she wanted and knowing he could not do it. Finally he said, "I've got to go back to Star City, but I'll wait until you find another man to work with Tug."

"We'll get married and I'll go with you," she said. "We'll meet whatever there is to meet and we'll do it together."

"No, I've got to go alone," he said. "I don't think there is much chance of me coming back, but I can't live this way wondering every day if one of old Bull's hired killers is waiting for me. I don't want to start running, either."

She sighed. "You're a stubborn, lovable man, and sometimes I think I hate you."

She kissed him, then he rose and walked to the door. He stood there a moment, looking back at her. He wondered how life could possibly deal a man a hand like this, with happiness right here waiting for him, and still tying his wrists so he could not reach for it. He said, "Good night, Sally," and went out the house and waded through the mud to the bunkhouse.

The next day Joe Veal rode out from town. He found Johnny and Tug Randall working on harness in the barn. He said, "Tug, would you go see if Sally needs some wood chopped?"

Randall grinned as he set a box of rivets on a shelf. "I chopped wood for an hour this morning, but I guess wood is something she can always use."

After he left, Veal said, "Damn it, Johnny, I hate to ask you this, but have you told me everything that happened when you left Star City?"

Johnny sat back against the wall and rolled a cigarette, studying Veal, who was plainly embarrassed. "I've told it all, Joe," he said. "I finally told it to Sally, along with saying I love her and want to marry her and I can't because I may be a dead man tomorrow."

"I'm glad you finally got around to saying it to her. My wife has been giving me hell because I ain't been giving you some. She claims Sally has about gone crazy waiting for you to declare yourself."

"I'm going back to Star City when the weather gets better and you can find a man to help Tug," Johnny said. "I don't know how much I can do except get myself killed, but I can't live this way. I'm not sure that declaring myself to Sally was a good idea. She may be worse off if I don't come back."

Veal nodded as if he understood. "I guess I'd better tell you why I rode out here today through the damn mud. I just got a letter from Sherm Balder wanting to know if you was still here."

"Does he want me arrested?"

"No. He's not sheriff now. That's what gets me. I'll

write and tell him you're here. Maybe he'll let me know why he was asking. Meanwhile I keep thinking there must be something I don't know."

"His term isn't out yet so he must have resigned," Johnny said thoughtfully. "He didn't say why or who was wearing the star now?"

"No," Veal answered. "I'll answer his letter soon as I get back to the office. I think you'd better stay here till I find out what he wants with you."

"I'll stay that long," Johnny promised. "You start looking for a man to work here."

He sat there a long time after Veal left trying to guess what had happened, but he couldn't. He wished he hadn't told Veal he would stay until Sherm answered his letter. He wanted to go back and get it over with, and he knew he would not feel right until he did.

− 1 9 −

By the end of April Dan Foley's nerves were close to the breaking point. Johnny Deere was alive and might come back. Foley had demonstrated to everyone and to himself, too, that he was not afraid of old Bull Tatum or the townsmen or any of the tough cowhands who came to town to raise hell. Many of them were bigger than he was and some of them had been mean drunk, but he had handled them. But now, when he was honest with himself, he knew he was afraid of Johnny Deere.

Foley had little resemblance to the man who had for years been the Pole Creek clown. He had quit playing practical jokes, he seldom said anything funny and did not laugh much when other people did. He had lost some weight and there were lines in his face. The worst of all was the pain in his stomach.

When he finally went to Doc Allen, the doctor examined him and shook his head. "You've got an ulcer," Allen said, "and you're going to have to be careful what you eat. Been drinking?"

Foley shook his head. "Not any more than usual. I never have been much of a drinking man."

"Well, you've got to avoid anything that hurts your stomach." Allen shook his head again, frowning. "Dan, it's my guess that something's worrying the hell out of you. Want to tell me what it is?"

"Nothing's worrying me," Foley said quickly. "I've got the job I want. I get along fine with old Bull, and Linda's promised to marry me. If I'm worrying about anything, it's the responsibility of taking on a wife and family."

"Could be it," Allen said. "Dan, there's one thing I just don't savvy. I've knowed you since you was knee-high to a grasshopper. I've seen the day when I wanted to whale you so bad I hurt inside. You and Johnny Deere were hell on high red wheels. There wasn't anything you didn't think of doing on Halloween. I know from personal experience, but you weren't mean ornery. Neither one of you. You were as friendly as an overgrown pup, and just as healthy. You started changing last summer and right now you're as different from the man you were nine months ago as you can be. Why? What's happened to you?"

Foley didn't answer for a moment as he pulled on his shirt and buttoned it. Finally he said, "Maybe it was Johnny having to leave the way he done. Like you said, we used to be hell on high red wheels." He buckled his gun belt around him and put on his hat. "Thanks, Doc."

As he strode along the walk toward the courthouse, he took a deep breath. It wasn't Johnny's leaving that was making his stomach kick up. It was the possibility that Johnny would return. If he did, Linda, even at this late date, might decide she wouldn't marry him, and old Bull Tatum would find out he'd been lied to.

The worst thing that could happen would be Johnny finding out that his father had not committed suicide, but had been murdered. He couldn't. Frank Deere was dead and buried. The coroner had called it suicide, and nobody was going to dig him up and discover that he had a bullet hole in his skull.

Still, if Johnny did find out. . . . Damn it! he couldn't, he told himself again, but one thing was sure. He had to go to Denver and find another man who would go to North Park and rub Johnny out.

He climbed the steps of the courthouse and turned into his office and stopped. A man was sitting down who apparently was waiting for him. When the man rose, he seemed to keep on unfolding. When he finally stood completely upright, he was the tallest man Foley had ever seen.

"You Dan Foley?" the stranger asked.

"That's right."

The tall man held out his hand. "I'm Logan. High-pockets they call me, but I never knew why." He laughed silently as if it were a great joke, but Foley failed to answer with even a small smile. He shook Logan's hand and dropped it, saying nothing. Logan said, "Funny, you being the sheriff. When I asked around town about where I'd find Dan Foley and they says go wait in his office, that being the sheriff's office, I was sure surprised."

"Why?" Foley demanded.

Logan looked around furtively, then said in a low voice, "Well, it just seemed damned queer for a sheriff to hire a man to kill another man. Don't you think so?"

Foley's blood pounded in his veins and he knew his face was red from the way it burned. He said violently, "Get to hell out of here or I'll throw you into the jug for disturbing the peace."

Logan held up a hand, a grin curling his thin-lipped mouth. "Don't get proddy, Sheriff. I can go see this

Tatum fellow and ask what happened. Or maybe it would be better if I started talking about your friend Bob Kregg."

Foley dropped a hand to his gun. He was afraid, so much afraid that his knees threatened to unhinge. He said, "By God, if you think I'll let you come into my town and start telling lies . . ."

"Not lies, Foley," Logan said. "Don't think you can kill me to shut me up. Won't do no good. I've got a partner camped up the creek who knows all I know. If I ain't back by sundown with what I came for, he'll be in town and he'll start talking."

Foley's hand dropped away from the butt of his gun. He laid a hand on his desk and eased around the corner of his chair and sat down. He stared at the mocking Logan, the thin, long-nosed face reminding him of all the pictures of the devil he had ever seen.

Finally he motioned to a chair. "Sit down, Logan. What is it you came after?"

"One thousand dollars," Logan said.

Foley's stomach was hurting so much he could hardly stand it. He leaned forward, his hands palm down on the desk. He said: "Maybe you don't know the salary the sheriff gets in this county. Where would I get that much money?"

"I ain't particular where you get it, Sheriff," Logan said. "I'll tell you how it is. I got purty chummy with Bob Kregg. One night we got to drinking and he told me why he came to North Park. He was to get a thousand dollars to kill Johnny Deere and so far he'd only got half. Well, me and my partner figured you still wanted the job done and we decided we'd do it for the same amount of money."

Foley stared at the desk top, but it was hard to see because little red lights kept dancing in front of him. He asked, "Who's your partner?"

Logan hesitated, then he said, "His name is Wash Smelser. He's wanted by the law, but I don't figure you'll be going after him, seeing as we'll be working for you. We ought to have twice what I'm asking because we'll divide the dinero, but we won't ask for any more than Kregg was getting. You see, we both have got our reasons for killing Deere anyway, but it seemed like we ought to get paid for it."

The fear was leaving Foley now. He fisted his hands and opened them again, staring at them as he turned this over in his mind. Logan had heard enough to know about the deal Foley had made with Bob Kregg. He wasn't the tough bastard Kregg had been, but if he had a personal grudge to settle with Johnny, he would come nearer getting the job done than a man like Bob Kregg who was completely indifferent in his feelings for Johnny.

"No, I won't go chasing this man Smelser," Foley said, "but I think I have a right to know why you two want to kill Johnny."

"No reason why I can't tell you that," Logan said. "I've been working for the Tuckers for years. The old man was ready to kick the bucket and I figured to marry the girl, but this Johnny Deere shows up and everybody began making over him and damned if the Tucker girl didn't fall in love with him. Maybe he don't know it, but I knew it, all right. When Bob Kregg showed up, he began asking where he'd find Deere, but nobody would tell him. I did. That's how he decided I was his friend and he could talk to me. Deere was gone on a cattle drive to Laramie, so Kregg had to cool his heels a while. When he did get back, he played his cards like a fool."

"What happened?"

"Kregg was a gunslinger, so he figured he'd get Deere into a street fight and outdraw him. It's legal murder and a man like Deere wouldn't have no show against a professional like Kregg. Only it didn't work because Deere didn't play by Kregg's rules. He started shooting as soon as he saw Kregg. I guess he'd been warned by the sheriff, a fellow named Joe Veal who was a friend of Deere's. Kregg started running so he'd be close enough to shoot straight with his sixgun, but Deere grabbed up a rifle and let him have it."

"Veal let it go?"

"Sure he did. He even told Deere he ought to have a medal. If Kregg hadn't let it get out what he was fixing to do, he could have jumped Deere at the right time and got him, but he told some yarn about his sister being wronged and he was there to get revenge for her death. Nobody believed him. For some damn reason folks in North Park think Deere is God's right-hand man."

Foley felt anger burn through him as it did so many times when he thought of Johnny Deere. This was exactly like him. He went to a strange place where nobody knew him, met a girl who fell in love with him, and the sheriff and everybody else started thinking he was God's right-hand man. It wasn't fair for Johnny to have everything.

Foley pounded the desk with a fist. He said hoarsely: "You've got a deal. Go back up there and do what Kregg didn't do, but go at it different than he did."

Logan's grin was quick and wicked. "We aim to. He don't have no rules to play by and we won't give him none. If you've got the money, we'll start riding."

"Wait a minute. What's Smelser's reason for wanting to kill Johnny? Is he in love with the girl, too?"

"No. I forgot to say she fired me when she heard I'd told Kregg where he'd find Deere. It was different with Smelser. Deere shot and killed his father and brother. Or maybe just the father. I ain't sure and neither's Wash, but it don't make no never mind." Logan rose. "The dinero, Sheriff. You'll have to trust us to earn it."

"You'll have the same deal Kregg did," Foley said. "Five hundred now and the rest in Denver after you've earned it. Get a letter to me as to where you'll be staying and I'll be there with the balance."

Logan opened his mouth to argue, then closed it and shrugged. "All right, five hundred."

Foley gave it to him and stood at the window as the tall man left the courthouse and mounted and rode out of town. Then for some reason he remembered that the name Wash Smelser was on one of the reward dodgers in his desk. He opened a drawer, took out a pile of them and thumbed through it.

Halfway down he found the one he had remembered: Wash Smelser wanted for attempted robbery and murder of Tuck Tucker and Sally Tucker in North Park. He grinned as he replaced the pile of papers and closed the drawer.

He put on his hat and, leaving the courthouse, walked along the street to the Hollison house. He couldn't let Linda put him off any longer. He had made her some fine promises about being the biggest man in the country. Well, he had a long ways to go, but he had started.

Now that he knew two men were going after Johnny, he didn't doubt that they would succeed. He remembered that he had felt that way about Bob Kregg, too, but now he was sure. There were two of them, and what was more important, he was paying them to do what they wanted to do.

Suddenly he felt like a free man, the first time in weeks. He saw Linda working on her hands and knees in front of the house in a flower bed. She was almost herself again, almost the old and lively Linda he had loved for a long time, aware of her appeal to men and proud of it.

As far as he knew, she had not flirted with any other man since she had promised to marry him, at least not the way she had when she had been engaged to Tom Tatum. When she kissed him, she let him know she wanted him as much as he wanted her. This was something she had not done when she had promised to marry him.

She didn't know he was there until he was halfway across the front yard and had called, "Linda." She rose and turned, dropping the short-handled hoe with which she had been digging. She swiped a sleeve across her sweaty face and brushed a hand over a rebellious lock of her hair.

"I'm a mess, Dan Foley," she said angrily. "Why are you sneaking up on me this way?"

"I love you, mess or no mess," he said, and took her into his arms and kissed her. "When will you marry me? Tomorrow? Next week?"

She looked up at him, smiling. "The fifteenth of May," she said. "I've talked it over with Mamma and we've picked the day because it's as soon as I can be ready. We'll live here for a while. Mamma will get a room in the hotel."

"Good," he said, and took a long breath.

It was his lucky day. He'd made arrangements for the death of Johnny Deere, and his girl had set the wedding date. He wondered what he had been worrying about. Johnny Deere would never come, he would be married in a little over two weeks, and he had old Bull Tatum in his pocket. Why, a man couldn't ask for anything more.

– 20 –

Mrs. Hollison announced that Linda and Dan Foley would be married May 15, and Dakota Sam Weeks made due note of it in the *Clarion* along with a lengthy and complimentary write-up of both of them, saying among other things that they were two of Star City's most promising young people.

A week before the wedding Mrs. Hollison brought Linda to Doc Allen for a complete physical examination. She had told him previously that she wanted him to explain about marriage to Linda, that it was something she had never been able to talk about to her daughter.

As soon as Allen finished the examination and Linda came back into the waiting room, Mrs. Hollison asked her to wait a minute. Stepping back into the doctor's private office, she closed the door and asked, "Is Linda all right?"

"Of course she is," Allen said. "I wish all the girls I look at were the picture of health that Linda is." He paused, studying Mrs. Hollison and remembering the history of her short and unhappy marriage. He thought about his own daughter Myrtle, and he said more harshly than he intended, "If you're worried about Linda's past, you can rest easy. I told her what she needs to know."

Mrs. Hollison stared at her folded hands that rested on her lap. "I'm relieved to hear that, of course, but it isn't what I really wanted to talk to you about. I've been opposed to this marriage right along, but you know how it's been with Linda. She's a very strong-willed girl."

She paused, close to crying, and Allen waited, knowing that she needed to talk. A moment later she went on, "I'm sure Linda never loved Tom Tatum, but she had her heart set on marrying him because of the money and position it would give her. Maybe she thought she had to make up for the fact that her mother was just a hotel cook. I don't know, but I think she did love Johnny Deere. I doubt that she would have married him, and I know how she tried to use him and then when it led to Tom's death, she thought she hated Johnny. Maybe she did. I've heard sometimes hate and love are very close."

She paused again, her gaze still on her hands. Allen waited, sensing she had not said what she really wanted to say and that she had come to the hardest part. She glanced up and, seeing that he was listening, lowered her eyes again.

"I don't know how to say this," she said, speaking slowly as if selecting each word with care, "but I'm afraid for Linda. A year ago she would never have agreed to marry Dan. In fact, she told me the other day that he had asked her once to marry him, and she had laughed at him. I don't think he's the kind to forget."

"No," Allen said. "I don't think he is."

"I suppose Linda has agreed to marry him because she wants to forget that she was responsible for Tom Tatum's death. Or maybe she thinks Dan will be important like Tom was, him being sheriff and all. Someday he'll inherit from his father and be pretty well fixed." She shrugged. "I don't know exactly what is in her mind, but that isn't what worries me. Why does Dan want to marry her? He'll hurt her, Doctor Allen. I'm sure he will."

He rose and walked to the window, not knowing what to say. He'd had a suspicion about Dan Foley for a long time, and his talk with him a week or more ago had added to the suspicion. Finally he turned to face her. "Maybe he will hurt her, but I don't see any way for you or me to prevent it. When you have a headstrong child who won't listen to you but insists on being burned over and over, there isn't anything you can do except to stand by and pick up the pieces if there are any."

He paused, and then added slowly, "I can't help you, Mrs. Hollison. I wish I could. I have the same problem in a little different way. But you've worked with Myrtle long enough to know about that."

She sighed. "I know, and I'm sorry. I haven't been able to help Myrtle, either."

She rose and left the office. He stood by the window until he saw them go past it on their way home. He should not have let his own problem come between him and Mrs. Hollison. She had raised Linda without the help of a husband just as he had raised Myrtle without the help of a wife, and both had failed.

He remembered what he had said about standing by and picking up the pieces; he remembered his suspicions about Dan Foley, too, and suddenly he realized that maybe there was something he could do for Linda.

He closed his office even though it was then only the middle of the afternoon. He stepped into Dakota Sam Weeks's print shop and found him asleep in his chair, his feet cocked on the desk in front of him. Allen picked up a newspaper, folded it, and slapped him across the soles of his feet, shouting, "Wake up. We've got a job to do."

Weeks almost fell out of his chair. He scrambled to his feet and shook his fist in Allen's face. "You son of a bitch, coming in here and yelling at me that way! Why, you could give me a heart attack."

"Chances are I will before you're an hour older," Allen said. "Get your hat. Let's go see Sherm."

Weeks grumbled, but he put on his hat and accompanied Allen to Sherm Balder's house at the north edge of town. Like Allen, he was a widower, and now that he had retired as sheriff, he had nothing to do but putter around his house and work in his yard. They found him spading his garden. When he saw them come around the corner of the house, he stopped work and mopped his forehead with a red bandanna.

"This the committee to control barking dogs at night?" Sherm asked, grinning.

"Maybe to control a dog," Allen said. "Can we go in?"

"Sure. I'll even open up a keg of nails."

"No," Allen said. "We need a clear head."

Sherm led the way through the kitchen into the front room. He motioned to chairs, then picked up his pipe and can of tobacco from a stand in the middle of the room. As he dropped into his favorite rocker, he said, "Shoot, Doc."

"All right," Allen said. "I've had this on my mind for quite a while and it's time I was telling somebody. I should have told it before, but I guess I was afraid to think about what it really meant." He cleared his throat, then he went on, "Frank Deere did not commit suicide. I called it that because I didn't think we could prove who did it, but the fact is he was murdered."

Sherm filled his pipe and tamped down the tobacco. He sat motionless, the pipe cradled in his hand, staring at Allen. Weeks muttered, "The hell!" and was silent.

"You'll remember his face was disfigured from a shotgun blast," Allen went on, "and judging from what Benny Quinn said, the way he found the body and the shotgun laying beside it, we jumped to the conclusion that he'd loaded it, held the muzzle in front of his face, and fired it with the big toe of his right foot. Well, he didn't. I made more of an investigation than I let on at the time. I'm a coward just like we've been cowards in this town for years. Now it's caught up with us."

"You still ain't told us how you know it wasn't suicide," Sherm said.

"He had a bullet in his head," Allen told him. "Whoever killed him shot him, then must have fired the shotgun thinking we'd never know about the bullet because of the way his face was chewed up."

Sherm put his pipe down. "Frank was my friend. I should have known he would never kill himself."

"I thought he just went a little loco," Weeks said, "living alone the way he did after Johnny left."

"Well, who do you figure did it, Doc?" Sherm asked. "Benny Quinn? He could use Frank's range."

Allen shook his head. "I think it was Dan Foley."

"Come off of it, Doc," Weeks said. "You're the one who's been eating locoweed. Why, Johnny and Dan were good friends."

"Now were they?" Allen asked, "I figure there's a lot we don't know. Maybe we never will, but let's think about Dan a little. You called him a clown in the *Clarion*. He had a reputation of being a practical joker. But we also know that old Bull Tatum insisted that Sherm appoint him deputy, and he asked Sherm to resign. We know that Tatum was responsible for Dan being appointed sheriff. We've all wondered what happened to change Dan. None of us know, even his folks. Now I'm wondering if he had this planned all the time and was just pretending to be a clown and to be Johnny's friend."

They thought about it a while, then Sherm said, "The night Tom was killed and we was taking Johnny across the street, Mrs. Hollison stopped us and said that what had happened was maybe Dan's fault and hers, but not everybody's. Now what did she mean by that?"

"I don't know," Allen said, "but she talked to me while ago. She said she thought Linda really loved Johnny, but she wanted Tom because he had money and position."

"There's another funny thing," Weeks said, "now that you think about it. That was the night Dan sort of took hold of things. Seemed like he wanted Johnny out of town more than anybody else. He even rode with Johnny for a while."

Again they sat in silence for a time. Presently Sherm asked, "What would be his motive for killing Frank? Let's say he hated Johnny because of Linda. I don't know what other reason he would have. Maybe he did want Johnny out of the way, thinking he might get Linda which it looks like he will. But Frank was as harmless as anybody in the country. I'm sure he never hurt Dan in any way."

"I don't know why he killed Frank," Allen said, "unless he thought Johnny might come back someday to see his father, and he didn't want Johnny around here."

"I've had some correspondence with the sheriff in North Park," Sherm said thoughtfully. "I haven't told anyone, but that's where Johnny is. I think I'll write to the sheriff again and ask him to tell Johnny to come home. We're going to need him."

"We need him right now," Allen said. "To tell him we were wrong about wanting him to leave, if for no other reason. We abdicated the right to call ourselves human beings that night. I'd like to have another chance."

"So would I," Weeks said. "There is one thing I'd

like to know. Why did old Bull want Dan appointed sheriff?"

"I'll ask him," Allen said. "I've been a coward too long. If you'll saddle up your horse, Sherm, I'll ride out there and ask him."

"You're wasting your time," Sherm said, "and you're running a chance of being hurt."

"I'll take that chance," the doctor said. "I was wondering about something else, Sherm. Why don't you write directly to Johnny if you know where he is?"

"Oh, I dunno. I just thought the sheriff might come nearer getting him to come than a letter from me would." Sherm looked at the floor for a moment, then rose. "I'll get the horse."

He was ashamed, Allen thought, just as he and Sam Weeks were ashamed, so ashamed that it was hard to even sit down and write a letter to Johnny Deere. It would be hard to talk to him when he came, if he ever did.

"I'll stay here, Doc," Weeks said. "I'll give Sherm a hand with the spading."

Allen was gone two hours. When he returned, he stepped out of the saddle and handed the reins to Sherm. "I didn't waste my time exactly," he said grimly. "He didn't tell me why he wanted Dan appointed sheriff except that he thought you were getting too old to do the job and he wanted a young man wearing the star. I asked why he picked Dan and he just said he knew Dan was available.

"But when I told him you were sending for Johnny, you'd have thought I'd blown the place up. He yelled that Dan had told him Johnny was dead. He wouldn't believe anything else, so I said we'd have to wait and see. Then he said that if Johnny was alive and ever came back here, he would kill him with his own gun, that he was tired of depending on someone else doing it."

Sherm and Weeks thought about it a moment, then Weeks said, "Johnny could handle old Bull. I guess what scared all of us was our notion that he'd bring his whole crew and take it out on the town."

"Jess Crowder was alive then," Sherm reminded him, "and he always depended on Jess doing his dirty work. Nobody seems to know where Jess went, but he's disappeared. Maybe old Bull knows. Anyhow, I think it's a good bet he cashed in and maybe Johnny done it."

"Strikes me that Johnny ought to know what old Bull said," Weeks said. "About using his own gun, I mean."

"It wouldn't make no difference," Sherm said. "I don't think Johnny was ever afraid. I think he left on account of he was worried about his dad."

"Or maybe because he didn't want to have anything to do with the likes of us," Doc Allen said, "and by God, I don't blame him. Well, I've got to get back to the office."

As he walked through the late spring afternoon, his long shadow moving beside him, he thought: *I didn't do anything for Linda. Nobody can. She's like a moth being drawn into the flame of a lamp. Nothing can save her.*

— 2 1 —

Near the middle of May Johnny and Sally took a Saturday afternoon off and drove the buckboard to town, Johnny because he wanted to see Joe Veal and Sally because she wanted to shop. They had no worry about leaving Tuck because he was up and around most of the day and could wait on any customers who came to the store. Besides, Tug Randall had chores to do around the barn and corrals, and would be within calling distance if Tuck needed him.

Johnny tied in front of the general store, saying he wouldn't be gone long and they could start back as soon as Sally finished her shopping. He started toward the courthouse. Joe Veal, seeing him, stepped outside and called, "Johnny, I want to talk to you."

"I'm coming," Johnny called back. "I want to talk to you."

When he reached the courthouse, Veal said, "Hell, I'd have saved my wind if I'd known that you wanted to see me. I just saw you out there in the street and thought I'd holler while I could."

"Don't make no difference about that wind you wasted," Johnny said. "You've got plenty more."

"Oh, I don't know," Veal said. "Some days I feel like I'm almost out."

Johnny grinned. "I'd like to see the day." Then his face turned grave and he said, "Find a man yet?"

Veal nodded. "Not a real good man like you and Tug, but he'll keep Tug company and maybe turn his hand now and then. Name's Luke Mimms. He's got a wife and a cabin full of kids. They're trying to prove up on a homestead west of town, and he needs some cash for grub, so he said he'd work a month. You'll be back afore then."

"Suppose I don't come back? Tug will stay on, but the Double T needs another man who can do more than keep Tug company."

"You've got to come back," Veal said grimly. "It would be the end of the world for Sally if you didn't." He hesitated, then he said, "Let's go into my office. I got a letter from Sherm Balder yesterday. That's why I hollered at you. I aimed to ride out to the Double T tomorrow, but you saved me the trouble."

Veal led the way into his office and shut the door. He sat down behind his desk and tapped his fingertips on the arms on his chair for a moment. Then, after Johnny was seated, he said slowly: "I hate like hell to tell you this, but I've got to. Balder wants you to come back. For some damn reason he thought I might have some influence in getting you to go back that a letter from him to you wouldn't. Your father died this winter, though I have a notion Balder has some other reason for wanting you to come back to Star City."

Johnny sat staring at Veal, not quite able to comprehend this. He had heard once from Dan Foley who had said his father was fine. But that had been two or three months ago. Any of a thousand things could have happened to him since. Living alone, he could have had a heart attack, or just got sick and died, being the kind of man who never wanted to be a burden to anyone.

Johnny did not doubt the truth of what Veal told him. He wouldn't lie and neither would Sherm Balder, and yet he could not fully believe that his father was gone. Not for a time, and when it finally worked into his consciousness, his sense of guilt was almost unbearable.

If he had stayed home, he might have died at the hands of old Bull Tatum and the Rainbow crew, and his father might have died with him, but he knew now with sudden and decisive insight that his father would rather have died that way than to be left alone all winter as he had been and go out without anyone there to let him know that he was loved and was not the complete failure that many people judged him to be.

Financial failure was not real failure. He had raised Johnny. Whatever virtues and strengths that he possessed he owed to his father. Now, seeing his past with the wisdom that had been gained in the months since he had left home, he wondered how he could have let the crazy recklessness possess him that night which had led to the death of Tom Tatum.

He rose. "I'll leave in the morning."

Veal got up and, walking to the door with him, laid a hand on his shoulder. "I'm sorry, Johnny. I lost my father years ago, so I know a little bit how you feel."

"Thanks, Joe," Johnny said.

"One more thing. Balder said that Tatum believes you're dead. When you go back, Balder thinks Tatum will try to gun you down himself. I don't know if it's important or not, but he also said that Dan Foley was sheriff."

At the moment none of this made any impression on Johnny. He said again, "Thanks, Joe," and left the courthouse.

When Sally finished in the store, a clerk carried her purchases to the buckboard and laid them in the bed behind the seat. Johnny was sitting motionless, holding the lines in his hands, his eyes staring at some distant point far across the park. Sally climbed to the seat beside him and touched his arm.

"What is it, Johnny?" she asked.

He spoke to the team, not answering until they

were out of town. Then he said, "Joe had a letter from Sherm Balder. My father is dead."

"Oh, I'm sorry, Johnny." Her fingers squeezed his arm. "Did he say how it happened?"

"No. Maybe it don't make much difference. He's gone. If I'd stayed home, he might still be alive."

"It doesn't do any good to blame yourself, Johnny," she cried. "You don't know. Maybe both of you would be dead."

"I know," he said. "Only thing is I suppose I thought that I could solve my problems by going off and leaving them. Well, you don't solve anything that way, so I'm leaving in the morning. A man named Luke Mimms will come out and help Tug till I get back."

"We'll be all right," she assured him. "Just be sure you come back."

That, he thought, was the last thing he could be sure about. They rode in silence then, reaching the Double T well after dark. No light showed in the bunkhouse, so Randall must have gone to bed. Johnny wondered about that as he drove around the house to the kitchen door. Tuck was still up because the windows in both the front room and the kitchen were lighted.

He carried the packages into the kitchen and laid them on the table, calling, "Tuck."

The old man hobbled out of the front room, a shotgun in his hands. "Where the hell have you two been?" he asked peevishly. "Sparking all the way home, I s'pose."

"Ain't that what two people in love are supposed to do?" Johnny asked, irritated by the old man's attitude.

"Yeah, maybe, only I ain't seen hide nor hair of Randall for two, three hours," Tuck said, "and I got scared. A couple o' men was out by the corral 'bout dark. One of 'em looked like Wash Smelser."

Tuck had seen young Smelser in every bush and ravine since he'd been out of bed. He kept saying that someday the outlaw would come back and try to finish the job he and his father and brother hadn't completed that day in Hogan's Hole, so Johnny wasn't worried. Still, he wondered about Randall. He had been told to stay in the house if Johnny and Sally weren't back by dark, and it wasn't like him not to follow orders.

"Grandpa, Johnny's father died," Sally said. "He just heard it today."

Peevishness fled from the old man's face. He said, "I'm sorry, boy. I sure am sorry."

"Thanks," Johnny said.

He drove to the barn and unhooked. Randall usually helped with the horses and asked about what was going on in town, but he didn't show up tonight. Johnny walked toward the bunkhouse after he'd taken care of the horses, wondering if for once Tuck had seen what he thought he had. Probably not, Johnny decided. His eyes weren't good and he'd said it was about dark.

Johnny dismissed any thought of danger until he reached the bunkhouse door, then he stopped with his back against the wall, his heart thumping with great, hammerlike beats. He'd caught the smell of cigarette smoke. Tug Randall did not smoke. He was probably dead and Smelser and whoever was with him were probably inside waiting for Johnny to go into the bunkhouse and light a lamp. Or maybe they intended to cut him down as he stepped through the doorway. He considered this a moment. The night was very dark, so the men inside would not have much of a target to shoot at when he went through the door.

He drew his gun. He was in no mood to draw this out. Besides, Randall might be alive and need help. There was a chance, too, that the second man was outside somewhere and might make an attempt on Sally's or Tuck's life, or both.

Johnny plunged through the door to the opposite side, letting out a great yell. He went straight on through so that his back was to the wall beyond the door. Two men opened up with their guns from the far end of the room. For some reason one of them apparently fired at the floor; the other laid his shots in close to Johnny's rapidly moving body, but the man's reactions had been a split second slow and the bullets missed by inches.

Johnny fired twice at the flashes of powder flame,

then he dropped to the floor as he heard one of the men go down with a great clatter. He must have struck the table and turned it over. The second man, who had fired at the floor, jumped forward and kept shooting, spreading his slugs from the door to the corner of the room about belly high on the average man. Lying on the floor, Johnny tilted his gun and fired the last three shells in the cylinder, then he moved swiftly and silently to the opposite side of the door.

He reloaded, listening for any sound that would give the other's presence away. Judging from the way the first man had fallen, he had been hit hard or was dead, but Johnny had no idea about the second. He had not heard the man groan or cry out in pain. He might be waiting for Johnny to give his position away.

The seconds ticked by, then Johnny heard Sally's feet pound on the hard dirt of the yard. He yelled, "Stay outside," and moved at once, expecting the man to fire at the sound of his voice. He didn't, and Sally came in, acting as if she had not heard Johnny's warning. He grabbed her and pulled her against the wall, standing in front of her so that his body shielded hers.

Johnny heard a man's ragged breathing then. It was as if he were laboring for breath, then he said hoarsely, "Light the lamp. I'm finished."

"It's Highpockets," Sally cried. "Let me go, Johnny."

He suspected a trick and kept his grip on her. He

put a hand over her mouth, whispering, "He tried to kill me. He may have killed Randall already. Now shut up."

She quit struggling. They heard the labored breathing again, then Logan's voice, "Light . . . the . . . lamp . . . I . . . wouldn't hurt . . . Sally."

No one could fake that sound of breathing, Johnny thought. The lamp had been broken. The smell of kerosene was strong in the room along with the odor of burning gunpowder.

"I'll strike a match," Johnny said, releasing the girl.

He moved forward past the first bunk and struck the match, the cocked gun in his right hand. High-pockets Logan lay on his back, his mouth open, blood drooling from the corners of his mouth. On beyond him close to the overturned table was the second man, a bullet in his head.

"Dan . . . Foley . . . gave . . . us . . . ," Logan began.

That was all he said. Johnny heard a gurgle as if phlegm had gathered in the man's throat and could not be dislodged. He caught Sally and carried her outside. He said: "That's nothing for you to see. Go into the house and tell Tuck it's all right. I'll take care of it."

She obeyed, crying as she ran through the darkness. Johnny brought a lantern from the barn. When he returned to the bunkhouse, he saw that Randall was tied and gagged on one of the back bunks. The two men on the floor were dead as Johnny had been sure they were.

He cut Randall loose, wondering how Logan had heard of Dan Foley. Randall sat upon the edge of the bunk, his feet on the floor and massaged his jaws until he could talk.

"I tell you, Johnny," he said finally, "I thought I was a dead pigeon. You fired five times, and there I was, lying on the bunk not able to wiggle real good." He grinned. "But I saved your life even if you don't know it. You see, Logan was standing at the foot of my bunk. I lifted my feet and kicked him, and by God, it worked. Looked to me like he put his first slugs into the floor."

"He did," Johnny said. "Thanks. Well, we've got to take these carcasses to town and clean up around here. Did either one of 'em mention Foley's name until right there at the last?"

"Not that I heard," Randall said.

He would probably never know how Logan knew about Dan Foley, Johnny thought. It was ridiculous to think about his one friend back home ever giving these men anything.

– 22 –

Johnny rode into Star City late in the afternoon of a windy day near the end of May. He had been gone nine months; it might have been nine days or nine minutes as far as the appearance of the town was concerned. The same feeling of death and decay was here, the buildings fronting on Main Street still needed paint, and the words WATCH STAR CITY GROW on the water tower above the cottonwoods were as weathered and hard to read as they had been last August.

He reined into the livery stable and stepped down. Al Frolich stared at him in the gloom of the interior of the barn, not recognizing him for a moment. Then he did, and he yelled, "Johnny Deere!" and held out his hand. "I didn't know you. You look bigger, boy, and by God, you look tougher."

"I am," Johnny said, and wondered if killing five men since he had left had put the stamp of toughness upon him. "Give this animal a double bait of oats. I've come a long ways on him."

"I'll take care of him," Frolich said, and hastily led the buckskin away as if he didn't want to be seen standing there talking to Johnny Deere.

He went to the courthouse first hoping to find Dan Foley in the sheriff's office. He had thought about this all the way from North Park, and he still could not make any sense out of it. For easy-going, happy-go-lucky Dan to take on the sheriff's job just wasn't logical. The office was empty. Maybe Dan was out chasing horse thieves. He almost laughed at the thought. Dan was more likely to be in the hotel bar telling the last joke he'd heard about the traveling salesman and the rancher's daughter.

He hesitated in front of the courthouse for a moment, then decided to buy a new shirt and get a hotel room and wash up. He was hungry, and one of Mrs. Hollison's suppers would go down mighty easy. He'd ask about Dan later. Someone would know where he was.

He bought the shirt, Pete Goken shaking hands with him. He seemed a little fearful, Johnny thought, and remembered that Al Frolich had given the same impression. He left the store, disgusted. He hadn't really remembered how completely old Bull Tatum had the town treed.

Everybody, and that probably included Sherm Balder and Dan Foley, would want him out of Star City just as bad as they had last August. To hell with them, he thought angrily, as he went into the hotel lobby. He'd been stomping his own snakes since he'd left and he could go right on doing it even if old Bull Tatum was a hell of a big snake.

No one was behind the desk, so he tapped the bell and signed his name. A moment later Harlan Spain came into the lobby from the dining room chewing on a piece of recalcitrant steak. He almost choked when he saw Johnny. His face turned red and for an instant Johnny thought he was going to run.

"Johnny Deere," Spain managed finally, and held out his hand. "Welcome back to Star City."

"Thanks, even if you don't mean it," Johnny said. "I don't figure to stay here long. Right now if you ain't boogered too much to have me stay in your hotel, I'd like a room."

"Sure," Spain said quickly. "Fifteen. It's on the street. We don't have no keys. Most of the locks have been broken. Go right on up."

"I'll be down for one of Mrs. Hollison's suppers as soon as I get washed," Johnny said. "Tell her to start my steak."

"I'll tell her," Spain said, and fled into the dining room.

Johnny climbed the stairs and turned along the hall toward the front of the building. Fifteen was a corner room and probably as good as any in the house. That wasn't much, he decided when he went in and glanced around at the scarred pine bureau. One of the brass knobs atop a post at the head of the bedstead was missing. Some of the wallpaper had been torn and hung in shreds. When he turned to the windows above Main Street he discovered that one of them did not have a shade.

For a time he stared at the buildings across the street. A man on one of the roofs could dry-gulch him the moment it was dark and he lighted a lamp. He didn't think old Bull Tatum would use that method, but someone else like Pete Goken or Al Frolich, plainly frightened by his appearance in Star City, might decide to get him out of the way before he brought old Bull's fury down upon the town.

He pulled off his shirt and undershirt, poured water into the basin from the pitcher on the bureau, soaped his body from the waist up, and rinsed off the suds. As he dried, he told himself he had actually forgotten how small and cowardly and little the men in this town were, forgotten because he had lived in a place where there was none of the decay and apathy that had destroyed the basic values of human life in Star City.

Now he felt an urge to get out of town that was almost a compulsion, Maybe tonight would be long enough to stay here. He'd see that old Bull heard he was back and the chances were Tatum would make his move by noon tomorrow at the latest. Meanwhile Harlan Spain would either find a shade to cover the window or Johnny would move into another room.

He turned toward the bed to pick up his undershirt when he heard a knock on the door. He pulled his gun as he called, "Come in."

The door opened and Mrs. Hollison slipped in and closed the door behind her. She said, "Johnny, you don't know how glad I am to see you."

He dropped his gun back into the bolster, embarrassed as he grabbed for his undershirt, but she crossed the room to him before he reached it. She put her hands on his arms and looked searchingly into his face as he said, "I didn't expect a woman or I wouldn't have hollered for you to come in till I had my clothes on."

She acted as if she didn't hear. She said: "You've changed, Johnny. I knew you would, but I didn't know how much you would change. You were a boy when you left and now you're a man."

"Correct," he said, thinking that she was more right than she realized.

"I know you can take care of yourself," she said. "When Harlan told me you were back, I wasn't sure. Harlan's gone to tell Doc Allen you're here. Doc will be along in a minute or two, and probably Sam Weeks and Sherm Balder will come a little later."

"Mrs. Hollison, I didn't come back to see . . ."

"I don't suppose you did," she said tartly, "but a lot of things have happened you don't know about. I don't think I know all of it, but those three men do. Sherm told Harlan Spain and me several days ago to tell him as soon as you got to town. The reason Harlan went after Doc Allen first is that he's the closest."

"Mrs. Hollison," he said, exasperated, "the only reason I'm here is to get . . ."

"I know," she interrupted. "Sherm said he'd sent for you and you know your father had killed himself, but . . ."

"Killed himself?" He stared at her so fiercely that she stepped back toward the door. "I don't believe it."

"Ask Doc Allen," she said. "I thought Sherm had

written that to you or I wouldn't have mentioned it. They'll all be here in a minute and I've got something to tell you first."

"I told Harlan to tell you to start a steak for me," he said, masking his face against the pain of guilt that stabbed him. Now he knew how his father had died and he was the cause of it. If he had been at home and his father had had his company through the winter, the loneliness and despair that must have been responsible for him killing himself would not have overcome him. "I'll eat my supper and then I want to find Dan and . . ."

"No," she broke in. "That's what I came here to tell you. Stay in your room. Dan will kill you if he gets a chance. Don't give him that chance. If you go to him thinking he's your friend, he'll have all the chance he needs."

He stared at her, wondering why she had gone completely crazy. To mollify her, he said, "All right, Mrs. Hollison, I'll watch out for him."

"You don't believe me, do you?" she whispered. "You don't know what's been going on. Two weeks ago Linda and Dan were married. Don't ask me why she married him, but she was eighteen and I couldn't stop her. I've been afraid for her ever since they were married, but so far she's been happy enough, I guess. I'm living here in the hotel so they can have the house to themselves."

"Linda and Dan married," he said, and grinned.

"Now what do you know about that?"

"That isn't what's important to you," she said. "What is important is that Dan is not your friend and hasn't been for years. He hates you. He thinks Linda really loves you and he's crazy jealous. She's found out that much in the two weeks they've been married."

"She isn't and I'll tell him when I see him," he said, thinking that Linda didn't know what the truth was and had lied to her mother.

"He won't give you a chance," Mrs. Hollison said. "I don't suppose you remember, and maybe you didn't even know, but before you left, Dan used to visit Linda during the week when you and Tom Tatum were working and wouldn't run into him. She couldn't stand him, but she didn't know how to get rid of him.

"Once he proposed to her and she laughed in his face. It made him furious, but he kept coming back. Then she had this quarrel with Tom about having a house of her own. That gave Dan his idea. He told her to use you to make Tom jealous so he would do what she wanted. That was why she did what she did. Dan Foley is responsible for Tom's death, not you."

It was crazy and fantastic and impossible, and he did not believe any of it. She saw that he did not and made a gesture of despair as she opened the door. She glanced into the hall and turned back to say, "Sherm and Doc are coming. Ask them."

She left the room. He heard her say something to the two men as she passed them. Then they were in the room, shaking hands with him, and for the first time since he had ridden into Star City, he felt that he was being sincerely welcomed back.

"I'm sorry we're slow getting here," Sherm said, "but Doc was at my place. Harlan found us there. He's still looking for Sam."

"Mrs. Hollison was just giving me the worst cock-'n'-bull yarn about Dan Foley . . . ," Johnny began.

"Hold it right there, boy," Sherm cut in. "It's true, but there's more even than she knows. When I wrote to your sheriff, I didn't know about your father . . ."

"She said be killed himself," Johnny said.

Doc Allen shook his head. "He didn't. Nobody in town knew except me. I told Sherm and Sam. No one else. We decided to wait till you get back. Your father was murdered and we think Dan did it."

Johnny sat down on the bed, staring at Allen and then at Sherm. Finally he said, "If anybody had told me I'd come back and find that people like you and Mrs. Hollison had gone completely crazy . . ."

"You can think what you damn please about our sanity," Doc Allen said hotly, "but tell me whether you're willing to listen or not? If not, we'll walk out of here and you can go find Dan thinking he's your friend and let him blow your head off."

"I'll listen," Johnny said.

They told him how they knew that his father had been killed, and what had happened during the winter, one talking and then the other, reminding him first how anxious Foley had been to get him out of town, even passing the hat for him, and how that old Bull Tatum had seen to it that he was appointed sheriff.

He began to believe then, for he remembered that Highpockets Logan had mentioned Dan Foley just before he died. He walked to the window and stared at the street below him as a new and terrible thought nagged him. Maybe, through some strange set of circumstances, Dan Foley had paid Logan and Smelser to kill him. He rejected the thought. It was simply too farfetched.

"There's no real evidence that Dan killed Pa, is there?" Johnny asked.

"No," Sherm admitted, "except that I rode out there the other day after Doc told me what he knew. I didn't find nothing in your house or the yard, but I talked to Benny Quinn. He told me that two days before he found your pa's body he saw Dan riding toward town. He doesn't think Dan seen him. He was down in one of them little potholes, and he just glimpsed Dan crossing a ridge and dropping into the next valley."

"Now that you know," Allen said, "you can handle Dan any way you think best, but there is one other thing we want to tell you. We're ashamed of the way we practically ran you out of town, at least me and Sherm and Sam are. We've already sent a man to tell Tatum you're here. If he's man enough to tackle you by himself, then it's your fight, but if he brings his crew with him, we're buying into it."

The doctor must have seen the skeptical expression on Johnny's face, for he added defensively, "It's hard to say it, but we need to do something to help us forget what we did to you last August."

He looked from one man to the other, and it struck him that the apathy and decay had not reached quite as deep as he had thought, that there was the beginning of regeneration here in front of him. He said, "I guess I could stand some help."

"Good," Allen said. "Now let's go get supper."

– 2 3 –

When they finished eating, Sherm said: "Johnny, you'd better go to your room and stay there. We'll hear from old Bull in the morning one way or the other. Tonight one of us will patrol the town, just in case he gets the idea of bringing the Rainbow crew with him and burning us out or some damn thing we don't expect."

Johnny grinned at him. "Sherm, last August I was used to being told what to do, so I'd have gone to my room like you said, but you don't really expect me to now, do you?"

"No," Sherm admitted, making no effort to hide the worry that was in him, "but I wish to hell you would."

"What do you figure to do, Johnny?" Weeks demanded. "Ride out to Rainbow?"

"I ain't that brave," Johnny said. "Or stupid, if you see it that way. You said you've sent word to old Bull that I'm here, so he'll make his move and I'm willing to wait for him to make it. Dan's the one I'm thinking about. You've told me things about him that's hard to believe."

"You mean you still don't believe what we told you?" Allen asked incredulously.

"Let's say I'd like to hear what he's got to say," Johnny answered. "All the time I've been gone I kept thinking that he was the one friend I still had here. It's kind of hard to think any different until I hear it from him."

"He'll lie," Sherm said. "He'll deny everything we've told you. He'll claim he's still your friend and when he gets a chance, he'll kill you."

Johnny nodded. "Maybe he'll try. If he does, I'll know."

"All right," Allen said as if he were giving up. "I guess this is something you have to play your own way."

"I'll see you in the morning," Johnny said, and left the dining room.

He walked toward the Hollison house in the thin-ning light, his mind on Dan Foley and Linda and what had been said to him tonight. Maybe he was foolish, he thought, to risk his life trying to make sure of Foley's innocence or guilt, foolish because he knew, as Joe Veal had told him, that if he failed to return to North Park, the sky would fall on Sally Tucker. He was filled with a great warmth when he remembered the number of friends he had there, friends who were concerned about him, more friends than he had ever known on Pole Creek.

Even now he was cynical about how much real concern there was for him in the minds of Sherm Balder and Doc Allen and Dakota Sam Weeks. He had a strong feeling they were thinking of their own sal-vation more than they were of his, perhaps even of the financial future of the Pole Creek country once they were rid of Tatum, who had become a sort of "old man of the sea." He shook his head, condemning himself for having so little faith in these men, and yet the thought that they were using him and had asked him to come back to be a tool by which old Bull Tatum could be destroyed would not leave his mind.

He turned up the path to the front door of the Hol-lison house and gave the bellpull a tug. His gun was riding easy in the leather, but he had no thought of using it. Regardless of how Dan Foley felt toward him or what he had done, it seemed fantastic, even ridiculous, to think he would open the door and start shooting.

The door opened, but it was Linda, not Dan Foley, who stood there staring at him as if he were a ghost. She whispered, "Johnny," and stepped outside and shut the door and leaned against it.

"Hello, Linda," he said. "I hear you're a bride. Congratulations."

She didn't say anything. She seemed to shrink against the door, her hands clenched into tight fists. Waiting for her to invite him inside, he stood looking at her. He found it hard to believe she was the same girl he had taken to the dance that fatal August night, the girl who had lied to him about loving him and wanting to marry him, the girl who had tried to use him for her own selfish purpose even to kissing him with the unspoken but passionate promise that she would give him much more.

She was paler and thinner than he remembered her, and she looked nine years older instead of nine months. But there was something else, something less tangible but very real. It was as if the spirit or the bubbling vitality which had always set her apart from other girls was gone from her. She was dead inside, he thought, and wondered if Dan Foley could have done this to her in the two weeks they had been married.

After a long silence she said: "I can't ask you in, Johnny. Dan wouldn't like it."

"It's Dan I came to see," he said. "After what happened the night Tom was killed, I wouldn't walk very far to see you."

She moistened her lips with the tip of her tongue, her gaze not quite meeting his. "I'm sure you wouldn't. I don't blame you."

"Is Dan in the house?"

"No."

"Where is he?"

"I don't know."

She was lying, he thought, and he wondered why Dan did not want to see him. Even if he had done all the things that Sherm Balder and the others accused him of doing, Johnny found it hard to believe that he had changed so much that he wouldn't make a show of being the old friend he had always pretended to be.

"I've heard some bad things about him," Johnny said. "I wanted to ask him if they were true. You'll remember we were always good friends."

"Friends," she said softly and shook her head. "It's not the right word, Johnny. Not for you and Dan."

She started to open the door to slip back into the house, but he caught her arm. "Wait," he said. "Doc Allen thinks he killed my father. Did he?"

"I don't know."

"When you see him tonight," Johnny said, "you tell him that's what I've heard. He may be carrying a star, but it won't make me no never mind. If I find out he done it, I'll kill him, Linda. You tell him that."

"I'll tell him," she said. "Now let me go."

He released her and she slipped into the house and slammed and locked the door. He stood there a moment, wondering if she had saved his life. If Dan Foley were all that they said he was, he had gone crazy in a coyote sort of way, the kind of craziness that, once started, could send him down the murder road again and again.

He might have been waiting in the hall with a gun in his hand, waiting to kill him if he had gone into the house. He could have pulled it off, too, saying that Johnny had forced his way into the house and he had fired in self-defense. Linda would probably swear to the lie. If she didn't, she could not be forced to testify against her husband. No one could prove it had been murder. At least three men in Star City would have to admit that Johnny had reason to kill Foley, and they might even believe he had tried to do it.

He walked back to the hotel, wondering if so many changes could ever occur again in such a short period of time. The apathetic appearance of the town was deceiving. It occurred to him that the next hours would bring either a rebirth to Star City or the final act that would herald its death.

Someday the rains would come again and farmers would move back onto the hard land. Even old Bull Tatum, as solid and rocklike as he was, could not hold the tide back, but when the settlers came, they might very well take one look at this struggling, dying little settlement on the bank of Pole Creek and turn away to found their own town somewhere to the north on the hard land. In time even the county seat would be moved.

He stepped into the hotel bar and had one drink. Harlan Spain was tending bar. He talked in a guarded manner as if afraid he might later he called on to explain to old Bull or Dan Foley what he had said. Curly Mike Malone came in, saw Johnny and shook hands with him and let him buy a drink, then he said with a great pretense of being affable: "Come in tomorrow and I'll give you a haircut, Johnny. Free."

"Ain't you afraid old Bull will see you?" Johnny asked.

Malone grinned. "Maybe we'll just keep it a secret."

"I guess I'll turn in," Johnny said. "I've come a long ways today and I'm tired. Besides, it looks as if I'll have a busy day tomorrow."

"You sure will," Harlan Spain said. "You sure will."

Johnny didn't say anything about the missing window shade to Spain. It might be just as well to stay awake tonight and see what happened. If he didn't light a lamp, no one would be shooting at him anyway. He lay down on the bed, keeping his clothes on, but in spite of all he could do, he could not stay awake.

Johnny woke with a start, the dream of someone running in the hall so real that he wondered if it had been a dream. He sat up in bed and put his feet on the floor, realizing that he had been asleep and probably for a long time. Something must have awakened him, and he thought of the dream again. Maybe someone had run along the hall.

He rose and, opening the door, stepped outside, his right hand wrapped around the butt of his gun. No one was in sight, but he saw that a door was open at the far end of the hall, a finger of lamplight falling on the floor. He heard a woman's soft moans, and the voice of another woman asking questions.

He started along the hall just as a tousled-headed drummer poked his head out of his door and, seeing him, asked in the irritated voice of a man roused from a deep sleep, "What's the racket all about?"

"What racket?"

"The racket that woke me. Someone was running along the hall. Sounded like a stampede of cows."

So it hadn't been a dream after all. "I dunno what it was," Johnny said, and walked past him toward the open door.

Mrs. Hollison, wearing a maroon robe over her nightgown, stepped into the hall. Like the drummer, she, too, had obviously been awakened from a deep sleep. When she saw Johnny, she said in relief, "I'm glad you're up." Then she noticed the drummer peering at her and she said harshly, "Go back to bed, Mr. Burns. This is no concern of yours."

He started to say something, but Johnny said, "You heard her. Now do what she says." The drummer glowered, then obeyed. Johnny hurried on to where Mrs. Hollison stood. He asked, "What happened?"

She glanced into her room, then shut the door and stood against it. She said in a low tone, "I'll tell you after while. Right now I want you to get Doc Allen for Linda. And watch out for Dan. Linda says he took his gun and a hunting knife and left the house to look for you."

"He knows I'm back?"

"He knows. Now go get the doctor, will you, please?"

Johnny hurried along the hall and down the stairs. He glanced around the lobby that was lighted by a bracket lamp above the desk. No one was in sight. The clock on the wall said five minutes after three. He had no idea it was so late. Dawn was only an hour or so away.

He stumbled through the night blackness toward the doctor's office. No light showed anywhere along the street except behind him in the hotel. The darkness was so complete that he passed the front of Allen's office before he realized it. He turned back and found that it was locked. He pounded on the door, but no one answered.

Remembering that the doctor slept in a back room that opened into the alley, Johnny made his way around the building. He reached the back door and knocked. A voice from somewhere along the alley called, "I figured Linda would run to Mamma and you'd come for the doc. Where's Johnny Deere? He's the one I'm looking for."

It was Dan Foley's voice, high and shrill but unquestionably his voice. Johnny hesitated, then he said, "This is Johnny, Dan. How are you?"

Startled, Foley demanded, "What are you doing here?"

"Mrs. Hollison sent me after the doctor. What did you do to Linda?"

"Still sweet on her after all this time, ain't you?" Foley demanded.

"No. I've got a girl of my own. I didn't come back to steal your wife."

"You're a liar," Foley flung at him. "First thing you done when you got to town was to come to her house to see her."

"I went there to see you, Dan," Johnny said patiently. "Not Linda."

"The hell you did," Foley jeered. "Good thing for you that you didn't see me. If she'd let you into the house, I'd have shot you dead. I've hired three men to kill you. I don't see how in hell they could have all missed."

"I hear you killed my father," Johnny said. "Why?"

Foley cursed. "How did you hear that?"

"Sherm Balder told me."

Silence except for Foley's loud breathing, then he said, "I don't know how he found out, but it makes no never mind. He's another man I've got to kill if he knows."

"Have you gone crazy, Dan?" Johnny asked incredulously. This was not the Dan Foley he had left last August. "What's happened to you? All the time I've been gone I thought of you as my friend."

"Friend?" Foley laughed. "I never was your friend. You're crazy for thinking I was. I've hated you since we was boys."

"Why did you kill Pa?"

"Old Bull wanted him killed."

"Why?"

"He was your pa. That's reason enough. For me, hell, I didn't want you coming back. I figured you'd hear some way and then there wouldn't be nothing to bring you back. I knew I wouldn't have no show with Linda if you was around. I wanted her. By God, I wanted her more than anything else in the world and I got her, but she loved you all the time. You won't want her now. I fixed that tonight."

So that was why Mrs. Hollison had sent him for the doctor. "You've turned into something worse than an animal," Johnny said. "Why, Dan? I don't believe you've hated me all this time. You couldn't have. You never had any reason to."

"I had plenty of reason," Foley said. "Even when we were kids you always did everything better'n me. You could throw farther. You could ride better. You could shoot better. People liked you better. That's why I turned into the Pole Creek clown. It was the only way I could get people to know I was around."

Johnny heard him draw in a long, ragged breath, then the words, shriller than ever: "Linda thought I was a clown the first time I asked her to marry me. She laughed at me, but she'll never laugh at me again. Now I'm going to kill you. Don't think the law will touch me because I am the law and old Bull Tatum is on my side."

A lamp came to life in Doc Allen's bedroom. In the meager ray of light that fell across the gray dust of the alley, Johnny saw Dan Foley's broad shape, saw his gun swing into line. He drew his revolver and fired an instant after Foley's first shot ripped through the thin wall of the building not more than six inches from the side of Johnny's head.

Johnny's shot came so close to Foley's that it sounded like an echo. It smashed his right arm and flung him around and knocked him into the dirt. Allen threw his back door open and yelled, "Don't make a try for that gun, Foley. I've got my Winchester lined on you. I don't figure Johnny will kill you, but I will."

Foley sat up, his face contorted by shock and pain, his right arm hanging awkwardly at his side. He cursed like a wild man, his hard stare on Johnny and then on Allen who stood silhouetted in the doorway. He screamed like a woman, "Go to hell, both of you," and leaned forward and picked up the pistol he had dropped with his left hand.

Allen fired twice, both slugs driving into Foley's chest. He dropped flat on his back and lay still. Allen said: "This was the one man you were soft with, Johnny. I couldn't stand here and let it go. He was too dangerous."

Johnny holstered his gun, thinking that Dan Foley had asked for death, then he wondered if Foley was the only man guilty of his father's murder. He asked, "Did he deserve to die any more than old Bull Tatum? Or me? Or you?"

Allen stared at him sourly. "That's a hell of a thing to say to me after what I just did."

"Mrs. Hollison wants you to come to the hotel to look at Linda," Johnny said.

"All right," Allen said, his voice still edgy. "Help me lug him inside."

Later, as he waited in the hall outside Mrs. Hollison's door, Johnny could not get the thought out of his mind that Dan Foley was no more guilty than his parents and brothers, than old Bull Tatum who had used him, than the townsmen, than Linda who had once laughed at his love for her, than he, Johnny Deere, who should have understood years ago how he felt.

First Harlan Spain, then Sherm Balder and Dakota Sam Weeks, awakened by the shooting, came up the stairs and asked what had happened. Others were coming, Curly Mike Malone and Pete Goken and half a dozen more. Johnny couldn't stand them, not any of them, and he walked past them without looking at them or saying a word. He went into his room and shut the door.

Presently Mrs. Hollison knocked and stepped into his room before he had time to call to her. She shut the door and leaned against it, her gaze on his face. She said, "Johnny, maybe I know how you feel."

He stood at the window watching the day being born out there on the prairie, the first dawn light working its way across the sky and steadily deepening until the sunlight touched the very tips of the cottonwoods and the water tower with its faded words, WATCH STAR CITY GROW. Slowly he turned to face her, asking, "How could you know?"

"Because I don't understand Linda any more than you can understand Dan Foley."

He nodded, thinking about that. He knew what she

meant. She probably did not understand herself. Or what had happened to her. Looking back, she could ask herself why she had left town to marry a man who had later deserted her, and why had the daughter born of that marriage turned out to be the headstrong girl that she was?

"No, I guess you don't," he said finally. "And I guess you know what I'm thinking. I just don't savvy how Dan could have turned out the way he did. I don't . . . I can't believe he hated me all the time since we were boys. We had too many good times together."

She nodded. "I'm sure he didn't, but once he made the turn that he did . . . once he decided to be big no matter who he hurt, he had to make himself believe he hated you."

She hesitated, then said: "I want to tell you about Linda. She says they went to bed not long after you were there. She fell asleep and when she woke up, Dan was tearing her nightgown off and cursing her. He accused her of reaching for him and whispering your name. He said she had loved you all this time. Then he beat her and after that he attacked her like an animal, she says."

"She'll be all right?"

Mrs. Hollison nodded. "The doctor says she will. Her face is bruised so she doesn't want anyone to see her." She paused, then asked, "What are you going to do, Johnny?"

"I don't know," he said.

"I have to go to work," she said. "You'll be down for breakfast?"

"After while," he said.

She left the room, shutting the door behind her. He turned to stare into the street where knots of men had gathered to talk about what had happened. He considered going to the cemetery to look at his father's grave, and of riding into the sand hills to see if anything was left of the sod house where he had lived with his father.

He put both thoughts out of his mind. His father lived in his memory, not in the graveyard; he remembered the sod house and that was the way he wanted to leave it in his mind. Then he thought of old Bull Tatum, big and hard and vindictive, and he knew what he must do.

− 2 5 −

Johnny ate breakfast alone at a side table in the hotel dining room. Most of the men who had tried to question him were there, too, lingering over coffee. He felt their eyes on him, measuring him as they pondered what he would do.

When he rose to leave the dining room, Sherm Balder came to him. He said, "We'll side you no matter what happens."

Johnny looked at Sherm and then past him at Doc Allen and Dakota Sam Weeks and Pete Goken and the rest. They seemed old and ineffectual, dreamers who were still hanging onto their wornout, stale dream.

There would be years when farmers would make a crop on the hard land to the north, but life would always be a gamble for them. On the other hand, cattle would survive even the dry years. But Johnny knew there was no point in telling these men that. They had hoped for a long time that the stockmen would be destroyed and the farmers would return, and they would die with that hope in their hearts.

"I don't think I'll need your help, Sherm," Johnny said, and left the dining room.

He stopped at the desk to pay Harlan Spain, then went upstairs to his room for the sack that held his shaving gear and a few other odds and ends. He returned to the lobby a moment later to find the men who had been in the dining room waiting outside on the sidewalk. They were all armed. None seemed talkative and every one of them was trying to hide his uneasiness.

Johnny didn't stop even when Dakota Sam Weeks asked, "What are your plans for this morning, Johnny?"

"I'm taking a ride," he said, and pushed through the knot of men and strode along the boardwalk to the livery stable.

His tone was curt, forbidding other questions, so the men who stood there stared at him uncertainly as he moved away from them. He had failed to notice that Al Frolich was not among them, but just as he stepped through the archway he heard Frolich say: "Watch out, Johnny. Old Bull's here."

So he would not have to ride out to Rainbow after all. He sucked in a long breath, feeling relief. The trouble would be settled here in Star City where it had started last August.

He saw Tatum at the far end of the runway, as big and massive and unforgiving as ever. He dropped his sack and moved forward, his gaze pinned on the Rainbow man. He asked: "Who have you paid to kill me now, Tatum? Your hired gunslingers never got the job done."

Tatum cursed him, then he said: "A man's a fool to think anyone else will do a job like this for him. That's why I'm here. I'll kill you myself. I'd have done it the minute you showed up, but I wanted to be damned sure you knew why you were getting it. You killed Tom . . ."

"And you're proud that you're the kind of man who never forgets and never forgives," Johnny said. "Let me tell you something, Tatum. I didn't kill Tom. That was an accident, but since then I've killed every man you sent after me, and that includes Jess Crowder."

He saw the man's face turn dark; he saw the wild

hunger in his eyes. There was this moment of silence, of waiting. Johnny, watching, sensed that old Bull Tatum was like a cornered dog, forced into this position by his pride and self-condemnation. He had lost Tom, then Jess Crowder, and finally Dan Foley. Now he must make a stand, convinced at last that it was better to risk death than to go on depending on men who failed.

Tatum made his draw, grabbing his gun from the holster and firing, the bullet digging up the litter that covered the runway. Johnny's first shot hit him in the chest and drove him back one step and partly around, but it didn't knock him down. He held to his gun; he stood there bringing it up slowly, calling on that great and stubborn power which had been channeled into making Rainbow what it was.

Johnny did not fire again. He watched Tatum's gun barrel tip down slowly, heard the blast as the big man pulled the trigger again and saw the spongy dirt in front of him lift with the impact of the slug. Then he went down in a great, sweeping fall.

Johnny holstered his gun, staring at the body of the man who had tried to buy his death and then had tried to kill him himself, the man who once had controlled this range and now was an inert mass of flesh and bone. He discovered with surprise that he did not hate him. He was just glad that it was over.

"Where's my horse?" Johnny asked Al Frolich who

had hesitantly stepped out of a stall.

Frolich's gaze was pinned on the dead man as if he did not believe what he had seen. He said, without looking at Johnny, "In the back stall on the right."

By the time Johnny had the horse saddled and was leading him along the runway, Sherm Balder and the others had gathered around the body, Doc Allen having examined him and pronounced him dead. Now they shook hands with Johnny, solemn-faced and triumphant, and somehow managing to convey the impression that they, too, had had a hand in bringing about the death of old Bull Tatum.

"There's some money coming to you from the sale of the stock and things that were on your pa's place," Sherm said. "There's a note that Benny Quinn gave for the land, too. If you'll come . . ."

"You've got my address," Johnny said. "Mail it to me."

"You ain't leaving?" Dakota Sam Weeks asked incredulously. "Why, this is your home."

They expected him to stay and marry Linda, he thought. Like the weathered words on the water tower, they had been here in Star City a long time. They would die and be buried here. They'd had this one flurry of courage when they said they would side him. Perhaps they would have, but still they hadn't really changed, and he would not forget what they had said and done in Sherm Balder's office last August.

He did not have the heart to tell them what he thought of them, that nothing had changed and it was not his home any more. No use to tell them, either, that on the other side of the Medicine Bows he had found the kind of people he liked, the tough and good and virile people who lived in a hard and sometimes cruel land and still had tamed it and made it give them a living, or that he had found an honest and straightforward woman he loved who was not at all like Linda.

"Yes, I'm leaving," he said at last. "North Park's my home now."

Sherm threw out a hand in protest. "But damn it, boy, we need you. You're the kind of man this country needs. Why did you come back if you didn't intend to stay?"

"You sent for me," Johnny said, wanting to question his motive in sending for him, but knowing it would only hurt him and do no real good. "Remember?"

"Sure," Sherm said, "but I figured you'd buy your place back from Benny Quinn and you'd settle here among us. Your pa's buried. Why, you ain't even been out there to see his grave."

"Pa's here and he knows it," Johnny tapped his chest. "He ain't on that ridge where you buried him. I'd made up my mind to come back before Joe Veal told me about your letter. I've learned several things since I left here. The most important is that your problems don't go 'way because you ride off and leave them. Tatum was hiring men to kill me. I didn't want to go through life wondering if the next man I'd meet was another one of Tatum's hired gunslicks."

He picked up the sack and tied it behind his saddle, then stepped up. He said, "So long," and rode out of the stable and turned west on Main Street.

He glanced at the hotel, thinking for a moment he should say good-by to Mrs. Hollison, then decided against it. She was the one person in Star City he respected, but nothing would be gained by seeing her again. She was born to trouble and her life would never change any more than Sherm Balder's or Dakota Sam Weeks's or those of any of the rest.

Then the town was behind him and the last resentment that he had held for so long over the way he had been treated last August went out of him. Here was the undeniable working of the law of cause and effect; he could look back and see the sequence of events that man calls fate.

What was behind was behind, and the future seemed very good indeed. He stared at the long, gentle rise of the prairie that lifted ahead of him, and touched his buckskin lightly with his spurs. He would stay at Fort Collins and ask if the pass was open. He did not want to go the long way around.

Mrs. Sally Deere! He smiled as he said it aloud. It

would be the first change he would make when he returned to the Double T.

Center Point Publishing
600 Brooks Road • PO Box 1
Thorndike ME 04986-0001 USA

(207) 568-3717

US & Canada:
1 800 929-9108